In that instant, a flash of green energy tore through Heather's body, crackling along the surface of her skin with that all-too-familiar itching sensation. She howled in chorus with the whippet's death howl in her mind, feeling its connection to life break with a *snap!* that sent her own head whiplashing back.

This time the howl was her own.

Heather whined, crazy from the itching sensation that enveloped her body. She scratched wildly — and saw that her hands were no longer hands. Even as she watched, her palms shrank, thumbs receding, fingernails pushing out to become hard black claws. Her arms were sprouting coarse brown fur.

She screamed, only to find that her vocal chords refused to produce sound . . .

SMALLVILLE™

#1: *Arrival*

#2: *See No Evil*

#3: *Flight*

#4: *Animal Rage*

#5: *Speed,* arriving April 2003

#6: *Buried Secrets,* arriving June 2003

Animal Rage

SMALLVILLE™

Animal Rage

David Cody Weiss and Bobbi JG Weiss

Superman created by
Jerry Siegel and Joe Shuster

LITTLE, BROWN AND COMPANY

New York An AOL Time Warner Company

First Edition

ISBN 0-316-17421-1
LCCN 2002111471

10 9 8 7 6 5 4 3 2 1

Q-BF

Printed in the United States of America

Chapter 1

Clark Kent straightened up and slapped the Kansas dust from his hands.

The sun was rising to midday and this was the last chore Clark had to complete before the rest of this Saturday was his own. Only fifteen, but well over six feet tall already, he felt so intensely alive that even farm chores were more an opportunity to utilize muscles and problem-solving skills than drudgery.

This section of the Kent acreage hadn't been planted in decades, farming costs being what they were, but Jonathan Kent was gambling on a rising demand for organic produce to justify opening up a new field. Test harrowing had turned up the rusting remains of a long-buried barbed-wire fence.

It was Clark's job to pull it all out.

He stared at the weedy soil and concentrated, focusing his eyes in a special way that he'd recently learned. The ground beneath him shifted and shimmered, then seemed to melt away as if transparent. Dense rock became gray smears, the earth itself a whisper of brown and tan. He felt as if he were standing on glass, staring down into the guts of Mother Earth herself.

There it was, starting about five feet in front of him and buried about two feet deep. Clark narrowed his focus to be sure. "Gotcha," he muttered.

He traced three long, tangled, glowing lines that looked like veins with spikes. That old barbed wire had once been a fence marking the separation between cultivated land and the vast Kansas wilderness. Now it was a hazard to the tractor that the Kents couldn't afford to fix if damaged.

Clark rolled up his sleeves and plunged his arms deep into the hard, dry soil, his uncanny strength allowing him to bully his way through ground that otherwise required metal-edged tools. His X-ray vision guided his hands to the glowing wires. He grabbed the nearest one in a fist, amused to feel sharp barbs that would stab normal skin actually bend back like rubber against his own invulnerable skin.

He began to pull. Like a fishing line being hauled back out of the sea, the barbed wire tore its way up through the ground. Pulling and walking through the field, Clark unearthed the rusty wire, coiling it around his forearm like it was nothing more than clothesline. Minutes later, the job was done and the wire was ready to join the other metal scrap in the pile behind the barn.

Satisfied with a job well done, Clark took a moment to gaze out at his family's farm. Hard to believe that just a few generations ago this land was an island in a wilderness. Harder still to believe that millions of years ago all this was at the bottom of a warm, shallow sea teeming with fantastical creatures. But he could tell they had been there. By stretching his special vision to its limits he could see their fossilized skeletons hidden deep beneath modern Kansas.

Fossils were only ancient bones slowly converted to stone, and to Clark's eyes, stone appeared as a ghostly blur. There were denser lumps in the soil, though, lumps with enough metal content to partially block his X-ray vision. Many of these lumps were much more recent than the dinosaur remains — and not of this earth at all. Twelve years before, a lethal stony rain had fallen on this part of the Kansas plain, bombarding Smallville and changing the lives of everyone who lived there, Clark's included.

Some of the meteors were the usual drifting space junk — stone, nickel-iron lumps. A smaller number contained exotic green crystals that seemed to have the power to alter the chemistry of living things that came into contact with them. And one of the falling objects was a space capsule that contained a very young boy.

Clark had been that boy. He had no idea where he or his capsule had come from, but as he grew, he found that he had abilities and powers that his playmates didn't. Some of these powers, like superhuman strength and speed, had shown up early. Others, like his latest gift of X-ray vision, had only appeared recently and still took some adjusting to.

The smell of the freshly turned earth filled Clark's nose, which seemed more sensitive of late. He could smell bales of hay and alfalfa stacked in the barn over half a mile away. He could smell the sharp tang of the lemons his mother, Martha Kent, was squeezing in the kitchen. He could also smell that terrible aftershave that his best friend, Pete Ross, insisted on wearing, even though Pete didn't need to shave yet.

Wait a minute — Pete's aftershave? In the house?

After checking to make sure no one was in sight, Clark sped back home faster than any other human on earth could run. Dropping the wire behind the barn took only a fraction of a second, and he reached his back door in less than three seconds.

"Clark," his mother's voice called through the screen door, "you have some visitors."

Clark didn't need his mother's hint to slow down. He had grown accustomed to hiding the special powers that made him different from everyone else. When he entered the kitchen, his four visitors only saw a tall, gangling farm boy ambling in from a morning of chores.

Seated around the kitchen table sipping fresh lemonade were his closest friends, Pete Ross and Chloe Sullivan — fellow freshmen and also fifteen. With them was Heather Fox, a girl Clark knew only slightly. She lived with her grandmother in the Fox family home near downtown. Rumor had it that her grandmother lived in a world of her own on the top floor and rarely came out, leaving Heather a virtual latchkey kid. Heather had a rep in school for her strident attitudes about the "criminal" mistreatment of animals by, according to Heather, everyone on the planet. Her book bag bore the sticker FUR IS MURDER.

A fourth guest sat off to one side, almost in the corner. Bald, with piercing green eyes, he wore an expensive sports jacket over a crisp, white, open-collared shirt and slacks with knife-edge creases. Only twenty-one, he had sped his way through college at an unprecedented pace and was already an important business presence in Smallville. Flashing a brief smile, Lex Luthor nodded a greeting to Clark.

"Time for you to wash off that dirt and change into your secret identity as ace reporter for the Smallville High *Torch*," said Chloe by way of hello. She cocked her head to one side, peering up at him from behind her blond bangs. "Now that you're here, our editorial meeting can begin."

"I'm not on the *Torch* staff, Chloe," said Clark, heading for the sink. "I doubt I'd make a good reporter. And isn't the meeting normally on Mondays?"

Chloe beamed. "Since you hang around the *Torch* office all the time, I've decided to put you to work. And to make that easier for you, I decided to move the meeting here."

Clark couldn't suppress a grin. Good ol' Chloe, always ready to do a guy a favor — whether he needed it or not. "That explains Pete and Heather, maybe," he said, drying his hands. "But you, Lex . . . ?"

Lex held up his hands, mock defensively. "I'm just an innocent bystander who happened to drop in," he said. "But I'd love to stay and watch, if you don't mind. LuthorCorp has a history of sponsoring worthy causes in Smallville — like next week's Lowell County Fair — and I was thinking it might be time for me to extend a helping financial hand to a deserving organization." He eyed Chloe. "Say, the *Torch?*"

Chloe met the young billionaire's steady gaze. "You'd have to talk to Principal Kwan about that. It's a school newspaper, after all, not a scandal rag like the Metropolis *Inquisitor.* Besides, surely megacapitalist Lex Luthor would want some return for his money?"

"Nothing but the satisfaction of helping my adopted community." Lex flicked some imaginary lint from the collar of his immaculate sports jacket. "Of course, I *am* fascinated by that Wall of Weird of yours. I'd love to be kept up-to-date on those kinds of things." Chloe kept a scrapbook of sorts — on the wall of the *Torch*'s Smallville High office — about all the strange and unnatural things that kept happening in the Smallville area. The Wall had grown, article by article, until it overflowed its original bulletin board and filled most of the available wall. Being only five four, Chloe needed a stepladder to paste the latest oddities up near the ceiling.

Chloe's eyebrows shot up into her hairline. "Since your father's fertilizer plant is suspected of being the *cause* of half those reports, mightn't that create a teensy conflict of interest?" She leaned toward Lex. "What if the *Torch* decided to do an exposé on a certain billionaire's son?"

"Well, Ms. Sullivan, I should hope never to be caught doing something that would merit an exposé in the *Torch*." A faint smile flickered at the edge of Lex's mouth. "Tell you what, though. If it *does* ever happen, I'll grant you an exclusive interview."

"Okey dokey, moving from verbal jousting to *real* sports," interrupted Pete, "I've got a great cartoon for my piece on Friday's Griffins game."

Grandville was the nearest neighboring town, and the Griffins were the Smallville Crows' traditional arch rivals. After seventy-two years of head-to-head competition, the Crows were now ahead one game in the latest football series. Everyone was looking for a big win against the Griffins to cement their lead. Pete, not much taller than Chloe, threw himself almost maniacally into any sports-related activity. He was buff and he kept his wiry black hair close-cropped to fit into his football helmet. He was determined to prove himself against all obstacles, particularly his sports-hero older brothers.

Pete held up a sheet of paper. On it was a drawing of an outhouse decorated with the Griffins' logo. Over the drawing, a slogan proclaimed GRIFFINS — WE'RE NUMBER 2, SO WE TRY HARDER!

"Prime jock humor," Chloe said dryly. "Sure it won't go over the fans' heads?" Before Pete could answer, she added, "It's in. Next?"

"I'd like to do a piece on the county fair," Heather piped up. Her voice always had a slightly shrill tone, as if she were filled with internal pressure like a teapot about to whistle. Her wild auburn hair was tied back today with a conspicuously hempen cord. The rest of her wardrobe — unbleached linen shirt, drawstring canvas pants, and Birkenstocks — strove for a similar statement of organic purity.

"Sounds good," said Chloe. "The county fair is always big news around here — especially since it's Smallville's turn to host it. Gives all the bigwigs a perfect opportunity to let everyone know how important they think they are."

"I was thinking of something more along the lines of an exposé," Heather said.

"Like, what really goes into all those Jell-O salads?" Pete quipped.

Everyone except Heather laughed.

"Be serious," she said. "Do you have any idea what modern factory farming does to animals? It's bad enough that animals raised for meat eat ten pounds of feed for every pound of flesh people eat — enough to feed all the hungry on earth — but the conditions they're raised in! It's inhuman cruelty! I want to write something like Upton Sinclair's *The Jungle*."

They all stared at her, at a loss for words, wondering what Sinclair's famous exposé on the horrific conditions in Chicago's early meatpacking plants had to do with their county fair. Aside from hearing about her strong opinions on animal abuse, Clark knew little about Heather beyond the fact that her family had moved from Smallville to Metropolis a couple of years back, but then, without explanation, had sent Heather back from the city to live with her grandmother.

Clark coughed gently. "I take it you have a problem with eating meat?"

Heather stared coldly at him. "I have a problem with cruelty to *any* animals," she said. "It's barbaric! It's nothing more than blood lust. It should all be banned."

Pete grinned. "I could live without the mystery meat the cafeteria serves but . . ."

"Don't make jokes about killing," Heather said. "We're supposed to be civilized." She sipped some lemonade, puckering her lips appreciatively before continuing. "You, Clark. You live on a farm. Don't you feel good working with the soil, raising corn and veggies . . . being so *natural?*"

"Well, we raise corn and organic produce, but —"

Heather cut Clark off. "Everyone should live that way," she said, shaking her glass for emphasis and almost spilling lemonade. "Why should we murder animals and eat them just to make profits for giant fast-food corporations who cut down rain forests?" Her gaze shifted directly to Lex.

"Sorry," he said lightly. "I run a fertilizer plant, not a slaughterhouse."

"But your father owns dozens of companies that exploit animals, and I'm sure he invested in thousands more to become rich. Wealth built on mountains of corpses!"

Lex's lightness disappeared. "I am *not* my father," he told Heather with a deadly calm.

Clark sighed in relief as his mother breezed in through the door. "Anyone for a snack?" she asked brightly, opening the refrigerator and taking out a plastic container. "I have some fried chicken here, straight from our own henhouse."

Heather dropped her glass. It hit the floor and shattered.

Chapter 2

The crash of breaking glass brought Jonathan Kent in from the backyard. "Is everything okay?" he asked, bursting into the kitchen.

"I thought you were good people. You grow organic," Heather gasped, jumping to her feet. "How could you raise little chicks and then . . . and then *eat* them?"

"Uhh . . . Heather . . . ," Clark stammered, glancing nervously at his father. Jonathan Kent could have stepped out of Grant Wood's painting *American Gothic.* His skin was weathered brown from daily exposure to the sun, and his hands bore the calluses and scars of a lifetime of hard work. Nearly as tall as Clark, he was a reserved, almost stern man who held to a strict code of behavior and expected others to do the same. Clark wondered how his father would react to this unacceptable rudeness from a guest in his house.

"Relax, Clark," Jonathan said. He turned to Heather with a kind but firm stare. "I'm a farmer. Farmers grow things for people to eat. Everything has to eat something else in order to live. It's the natural cycle. We try to keep things as *natural* as possible on our farm — and we try not to be cruel. You may choose to idealize nature, but up close, it isn't always pretty."

Heather opened her mouth to speak, but Jonathan held up a finger to silence her. He went on.

"Our chickens have free run of our cornfields after it grows high enough. That keeps them healthy. Since they eat insects, we don't have to use pesticides. That keeps us — and the land — healthy. We have cows to give us milk and butter. But when they get old, I sell the animals. Things would get pretty ugly here if I just let them die in the fields, don't you think? Besides, every bit of food we produce for ourselves from the farm is one less dollar spent — dollars we can't spare."

Heather's mouth tightened into a bloodless line and her body, rigid with righteous anger, trembled. She bolted from the kitchen, slamming the screen door behind her.

Pete was the first to break the awkward silence. "You want a do-gooder project," he muttered to Lex, "get her some heavy therapy — or her own rubber room."

"I remember her father now," said Lex, calm as ever as he stared out the door. "A fellow named Rufus Fox who got promoted to head a division at LuthorCorp in Metropolis. Quite the trophy hunter. My father lets him weekend at his hunting lodges as performance perks." He smiled reassuringly at Jonathan Kent. "Not my idea of recreation and, quite obviously, not Heather's."

As if to close the topic, Chloe said, "I think we'll pass on lunch, Mrs. K."

"If you're sure . . . ," Martha Kent said absently. Of all of them, she seemed most disturbed by the incident. She looked down at the container in her hands, then back at the door. Then she put the container back into the refrigerator and, after exchanging a look with her husband, they both headed into the living room.

Nobody spoke for a long while. Chloe twirled strands of her blond hair around a finger, pointedly *not* looking at the door, while Pete kept shaking his head. Lex, as usual, watched everyone else through half-lidded eyes. Clark was wondering how to break the uncomfortable mood when his nose suddenly caught a familiar scent of lilac wafting in on the breeze. Seconds later, delicate footsteps crunched along the gravel outside.

"Heather's coming back?" Chloe asked, puzzled.

"Maybe she rounded up an army of killer bunnies from the garden and is coming to teach us the error of our ways," joked Pete.

A feminine figure appeared at the screen door. China-doll petite, with dark brown hair and exotic, almond-shape hazel eyes, the very sight of her made Clark's heart twist in his chest. "Is this a bad time?" Lana Lang called into the kitchen. "I just saw a very upset girl running down the road."

Clark moved quickly to open the door. Was it

his imagination, or did Lana's lilac perfume seem more intense today? In spite of all his special abilities, he felt awkward and could barely breathe in her presence at the best of times. Now her perfume went straight to his head and filled his mind with bittersweet thoughts. No matter how he felt, Lana was in love with Smallville High's star football player, Whitney Fordman, and Clark felt honor bound to respect her feelings.

"You just missed a head-on crash between an eco-purist and reality," said Chloe. She gave Lana a wry grin. "You want to write an article for the next *Torch?* We seem to have a sudden opening."

Lana stepped into the kitchen, her eyes still a bit sun blinded. "Lord, no," she said to Chloe's general direction. "My Aunt Nell roped me and Whitney into emceeing the LuthorCorp public speaking contest at the fair. I have a ton of preparing to do. Speaking of which — I saw Lex Luthor's car outside?"

"Present and accounted for," said Lex from his corner. "I promised Nell I'd drive you to the meeting." To the rest of the room he explained, "I'm letting Nell use space at the mansion for her Planning Committee."

"Can't let a forty-room mansion go to waste," said Chloe. In spite of the fact that Lex was the most powerful man in Smallville and her own father's boss to boot, Chloe was determined not to treat him any differently from anyone else.

"Forty rooms. Is it that many?" Lex shrugged affably. "I lose count."

Clark thought about the huge Luthor mansion, amazed as ever that Lex could take such a sprawl of pure luxury for granted. In a fit of ego, Lionel Luthor had arranged for the ancestral castle to be transported from Scotland, stone by stone, and rebuilt in the middle of a huge estate out on Beresford Road. It had become Lex's home since his father had assigned him — exiled him, in Lex's own words — to Smallville to take over LuthorCorp Fertilizer Plant Number 3. Clark had visited the mansion many times now, but he couldn't imagine living in it.

Lex only smiled at Chloe's comment.

Lana's pretty face flushed with sudden embarrassment. "I have a strange favor to ask of you guys."

Chloe pretended to be insulted. "Did I suddenly become neuter?"

"I meant the guy guys," Lana said, grinning. "I can see that explanations would only dig my hole deeper. Just bear with me for a sec, will you?"

She walked up to Pete, bent close, and sniffed delicately. She obviously didn't care for what she smelled but covered it politely. "Not . . . that," she said, moving on to Clark. "And you're not wearing any." She approached Lex and sniffed again. "Mmm, that's nice."

"Suddenly I'm glad I'm not involved in this," Chloe said as she watched. "After the Heather scene, I'm almost afraid to ask what you're doing."

Lana giggled. "Sorry. Whitney's being a macho jerk about the fair thing. He says he hasn't got time to get 'fancied up' for it, and if I want him in anything but his jeans and letter jacket, well, that's my job. Can you imagine? Anyway, I'm looking for ideas in the way of a nice aftershave or cologne. I like Lex's."

"Thank you," Lex responded. "I have it made specially by a chemist."

"Great," said Lana. "Where can I get some?"

It was Lex's turn to look briefly uncomfortable. Of course, on him, it was the briefest flash before his customary smoothness slipped back into place. "Well, the truth is, you can't. It wouldn't smell the same on Whitney." He added quickly, "It's not an ego thing, it's purely chemical. The best colognes and perfumes are a matchup between scents and personal pheromones. What I wear is made up for me alone, based on my unique chemistry. I believe that a person should be as individual and distinctive as possible, in behavior and in presence. I like to stand out from the crowd."

"Now that's news," said Chloe.

Lex shot her a schoolboy grin. *Shy* and *retiring* were never words that came to mind when anyone thought of either Lex or his father, and Lex knew it. "So," he finished to Lana, "if you have something with Whitney's sweat on it, my guy could whip up something, say, in a couple of weeks?"

Lana shook her head wryly. "Not an option, I'm

afraid. I guess it's whatever they have in the Formal Shoppe for me." Smallville lived up, or down, to its name. It didn't have a mall, so anyone wanting to dress up without traveling to Metropolis made do with the we've-got-everything-you'll-need claim offered by the Smallville Formal Shoppe.

"You should take Clark with you, then," said Lex, a mischievous twinkle in his eye. "He has a rustic nose, undulled by city life." Ignoring Clark's look of surprise, Lex glanced at his Rolex. "But some other time, since we have to go now, or you'll be late for the meeting."

Lex and Lana made their good-byes and left. Clark watched them go, Lana's scent leaving him feeling heady with longing. In contrast, Lex's comment disturbed him.

Months earlier, Clark had saved Lex's life when Lex's Porsche had blown a tire, plowed through a bridge railing, and plunged into the river. The Porsche had also hit Clark at sixty miles an hour and smashed him through the same railing and into the river. Lex didn't know this additional fact, just as he didn't know that

Clark, unharmed by the accident, had ripped the Porsche's roof open with his bare hands to drag Lex to safety.

Lex claimed that his near-death experience had changed his life. His actions seemed to support those words. He'd pursued a friendship with Clark that was growing closer all the time, and Clark had to admit that it was nice to have such an interesting — and resourceful — friend. Usually Lex treated Clark as an equal, despite their age difference, but sometimes he adopted a sophisticated older-brother attitude, urging Clark to broaden his horizons and become more ambitious. Either way, they got along great — except when it came to Lana. She was the one point of disagreement between them. Clark was uncomfortable about the way the twenty-one-year-old tried to push him and Lana together despite Lana's current attraction to Whitney. Clark appreciated Lex's good intentions, but it still made things . . . difficult.

Chloe was riffling through her papers, unaware of Clark's inner turmoil. "This is great," she was saying. "Lana reminded me about the speech contest. I'm gonna have a field day with the topic that Lionel Luthor picked."

"Lex's dad got to set the topic?" said Pete.

"You put up five thousand dollars for the prize, you get to set the topic," said Chloe. "Money doesn't talk, it screams, as a pop poet once said. Ah, here it is . . . 'Man, Conqueror of the Wild.' *Trés* pompous, if you ask me. I can't wait to hear the oratorical gems *that* produces."

"Good thing Heather's gone," said Clark, only half listening. "Sounds like something that would really drive her nuts."

Chapter 3

Monday's classes were done, but Clark was still roaming the halls of Smallville High School that afternoon. Chloe had failed to maneuver him into writing an article for the *Torch,* so instead she'd "loaned" him to Lana as an assistant to Nell's Planning Committee. That way, she'd be able to write a story on the public speaking contest based on Clark's insider info. "I'll make a reporter out of you yet" was becoming her mantra.

The trade-off went as smoothly as any sports-club swap. That is to say, the owners made the deal without consulting the traded player. Clark sometimes wondered if all women simply presumed they could run the lives of the men around them. *Why does a guy do just about anything when a girl bats her eyes?* he wondered dismally. Then he remembered Lana's eyes. The cute way the corners crinkled when she smiled. The tiny gold flecks in her irises. Her long lashes. How he could just look into them for hours on end —

Smack!

Any other teenager would have felt the impact of walking face first into a wall, but Clark didn't even rub his nose. Instead, he glanced up and down the hallway to see if anyone had witnessed the stupid thing he'd just done.

The coast was clear.

He sighed in relief. *Okay, Clark, you're hanging posters,* he reminded himself. *Hanging posters, hanging posters — not daydreaming over Lana and walking into walls.*

He chose a prime spot at the T-junction of two hallways, between a row of lockers and a classroom door. He pulled out a poster from the fat folder Nell had given him and placed tape at its corners. The Planning Committee had designed and printed several different posters, each advertising different county fair events. This one read:

GOT BEEF?

CHOOSE THE BEST AT THE

LIVESTOCK AUCTION ON SUNDAY

OR CATCH YOUR OWN AT THE RODEO!

Clark figured that a half ton of angry bull had a definite advantage in any contest, even against him with his superstrength and speed. Still, there were easily a dozen guys at the school who highly overestimated their macho prowess. *Should make for some laughs,* he mused. *At least Pete's not cocky enough to sign up for it.*

Just as he raised the poster he noticed an electrical switch box in the way. Covering something essential, like circuit breakers or power junctions, its access door had a sturdy lock to keep prying hands out. There was nothing for Clark to do but hang this poster above it, still a good spot but much higher than he could possibly reach.

If he were normal.

He let his senses search the immediate area. No smell or sound of anyone in any direction, at least not nearby. Plenty of time. His knees tensed . . .

he leaped . . . he slapped . . . and the poster was hanging ten feet up on the wall.

Clark stood back and admired his handiwork. "Go, Kent," he murmured.

He moved to pick up the remaining posters and tape, then paused. Something . . . a strange odor . . . there one moment, now it was gone. He sniffed at the air, wondering.

He was getting used to having X-ray vision by now, but his nose was another thing. It hadn't dropped out of overdrive since Saturday when Lex had so blithely defined it as rustic. The word amused and irritated Clark at the same time. By rustic, Lex had no doubt meant a gentle jab at Clark's farm upbringing. But what Lex didn't know — what no one knew — was just how sophisticated his nose had recently become.

Take this morning at school, when he felt like he wasn't so much walking to classes but pushing his way through air that was practically soupy with clashing smells: perfumes, colognes, after-shaves, sweaty gym clothes, biting chemical odors wafting from the chemistry lab — how was he supposed to function in that chaos? Taking a simple science pop quiz had been agony because the girl sitting in front of him was wearing bubblegum lip gloss that reeked so badly it made his sinuses ache. And he was dying to tell one of Whitney's jock friends that deodorant had been invented for a reason, but decided it wouldn't be worth the fuss. *Let's not even think about the cafeteria,* he mused, remembering how the mysterious aromas wafting out of the kitchens had made him question his ability to ever eat there again.

He suddenly inhaled, nostrils flaring, his instincts startling him out of his reverie. There it was again, that weird odor — hot. Like burning. That was it — burning — ozone and burnt plastic! Clark had worked on enough farm equipment to recognize the smell of an electrical short.

But where was it? He squinted slightly to kick in his X-ray vision and scanned the light fixtures up and down the hall. Nothing wrong there. Another wave of the odor drew his attention to the access door in front of him.

The short was right there, behind the locked

metal door. Whoever had last serviced the wiring had nicked the insulation on a couple of wires and crimped them together. Clark saw tiny arcs of electricity leaping between the exposed copper strands. The plastic wrapping was melting and beginning to smoke. If he didn't do something about it, the wall would be engulfed in flames within minutes.

But how to stop it? There wasn't time to alert anyone else — the wall would be on fire before he got back. He had the strength to rip open the access panel with his bare hands — but that would leave evidence he wouldn't be able to cover up afterward. There was only one way he could pull this off without exposing his powers.

Clark's parents disapproved of his habit of carefully biting his fingernails, but the truth was, no tools but his own teeth were strong enough to trim his superdense nails. He'd never thought of using those nails as tools themselves. *No time like the present,* he thought, and fitted his right thumbnail into the slot of one of the corner screws. He twisted his wrist back and forth at superspeed, caught the screw as it popped out, and moved to the next one. Four seconds and four screws later, he had the access door off the wall.

Now came the tricky part. These wires ran 220-volt current — twice house current, which was deadly enough to ordinary people. Clark had never deliberately tested his seeming invulnerability against that much electricity, but now wasn't the time to hesitate. He grabbed a wire in each hand and pulled them apart.

His hair stood straight out from his head, and he could feel the soles of his shoes begin to melt as the powerful current tried to ground itself through his feet. But other than that, all he felt was a tingly buzz along his skin, as if an army of ants were marching over him.

His thumbs moved in a blur as they smoothed the molten insulation over the exposed copper. He pressed the wiring back into place, then hoisted the steel door back into position and replaced the screws. One, two, three, four. It was done. He stepped back.

"Are you proud of what you're doing?" a shrill voice said behind him.

Clark spun around. Heather Fox stood there,

her face twisted and angry. "Huh?" was all he could find to say. Had she seen his super fix-it job?

"Not satisfied with being an animal murderer yourself?" Heather pointed an accusing finger. "Do you have to brag about your cruelty? Make a *display* of it?"

Clark slowly realized that Heather was pointing at the poster, not at him. She hadn't seen him use his powers.

"It's the county fair, Heather," he said, noticing how her outstretched hand was trembling, she was so angry. "They hold it every year. And I'm working with the public speaking competition, not the livestock."

"I'm talking about that competition. Why didn't you and Lionel Luthor just call the topic 'Man, *Killer* of Wild Animals?'" Her face was turning red, lips curled back in an angry snarl. If she were an older person, Clark would have been worried about her having a stroke.

"Calm down, Heather," he said, truly concerned. "I haven't got a clue what you're talking about —"

"A likely story," Heather spat. "Next you're going to say that you don't know that Luthor is providing a special backdrop for the speeches. A backdrop of the murdered, skinned, and stuffed pelts of all the rare animals he's ever hunted."

"Well, actually —"

"Don't bother denying it, Clark," Heather interrupted. "Someday the animals are going to find a way of making *you* feel what they feel. We'll see how *you* like being the hunted one then!" Heather glared at him, panting. Then she tore away down the hall.

ꙮꙮꙮꙮ

"About this theme your dad chose . . ."

The confrontation with Heather had left him so unsettled that when Clark spotted the silver Porsche Boxster parked outside the Beanery, he'd ducked into the coffee hangout. He'd found Lex sitting at a back table, skimming several magazines simultaneously.

"Didn't he realize how . . . *tasteless* it would

appear?" Clark prompted when Lex didn't answer right away.

"Have you ever read Ernest Hemingway?" Lex finally said without looking up. His habit of answering a question with a seemingly unrelated question was growing familiar to Clark, as was his apparent ability to do several things at once.

"Sure," Clark answered. "*The Old Man and the Sea* is on the required reading list, but I read it way back in —"

"That's a good example to start with," interrupted Lex, closing the magazines and finally looking up at Clark. "My father is a great fan of Hemingway. He considers him one of the few fiction writers worth reading — not because of style, but because Hemingway's view of life reflects his." He raised his hand. Like magic, a waitress appeared. She set an espresso in front of Lex and a foaming latte in front of Clark.

"I love a waitress who remembers everyone's favorite coffee," Lex said. He smiled and pressed a twenty into the waitress's hand. "Keep the change."

Lex took a sip of espresso from the tiny cup, closing his eyes as if savoring the rush of caffeine flowing into his system. "My father believes that life is the arena in which a man proves himself against everything that the universe can throw against him," he said. "Conquer it or die. To him it makes no difference if his opponent is Nature, a wild animal, a business competitor, or a maître-d' at a restaurant. They're all the same — challenges to be beaten. Triumph is everything. With that philosophy, trophies are the badges of one's strength."

"But to get in people's faces by setting up a display of mounted hunting trophies" — Clark paused, swirling the latte in his cup and watching the froth melt into tangled spirals — "endangered species, no less. Is that an appropriate backdrop for an innocent speech competition?"

"Nothing is innocent, Clark." A hint of a smile lifted the corners of Lex's mouth as he leaned back into the overstuffed chair, clasping his hands behind his head. "Can't you see it from his point of view? It's completely consistent. Winning a speech competition — beating the competition, whatever the game — is just another way of proving you're the top predator. The meanest SOB in the jungle, with the pelts to prove it.

"And really, Clark, you have to admit it, there are a lot of people who will be at that fair — women as well as men — who will admire what it took to win those trophies and fantasize about doing it themselves." Lex's green eyes flashed with challenge. "Don't you?"

"Me? Of course not."

Saying that made Clark squirm, not because Lex was right but because he had nailed one of Clark's major dilemmas dead center. Ever since Clark had begun to display extraordinary strength as a young child, his father had drilled into him over and over what kind of damage he could accidentally do to innocent playmates. Jonathan Kent's strictness had extended to forbidding his son from participating in any kind of team sports, no matter how much Clark had begged him. Even now Clark hated knowing that his peers presumed him to be a wuss because he always sat on the sidelines of school life.

Still, he had to admit that his father's fears were justified. As much as he burned to defy family restrictions and prove to his friends that he wasn't a total geek, he knew the truth — if he ever lost control, even for an instant, for whatever reason, someone else's life could be in jeopardy. However much he hated the shame, Clark knew that he wouldn't be able to live with himself if he ever slipped up.

By instinct, Lex seemed to sense Clark's inner turmoil. "Oh, come on," he prodded. "High school is all about proving you're special, that there's something unique about you, that you're somehow *better* than those other guys. Why else would a shrimp like Pete Ross go out for football and basketball? And tell the truth, Clark. If you *were* better, if you *knew* you could whip all comers without breaking a sweat — wouldn't you do it?"

Clark saw a strange light in Lex's eyes as he said this. Lex had suspected there was something "super" about Clark since the accident. Was this another probe? Was Lex trying to get him to betray his secret?

Or was it something else entirely?

Clark studied Lex for a moment, his seemingly unshakable confidence, his air of casual superiority. The young Luthor was ever on the prowl, even when he appeared to be unconcerned. *No,* Clark thought, *especially when he appears to be unconcerned.* And at that moment, Clark realized something. Suddenly he saw beyond the face of this strange young man who worked so hard to be his friend. He saw the face of someone who had earned double university degrees with honors — without breaking a sweat. He saw a young man who ran with national and international power brokers. He saw a genius who was determined not to let *anything* in the world stand in his way, not even his own incredibly domineering father.

Was Lex talking about Clark — or about himself?

He realized that he owed Lex an honest answer. He looked away and thought deeply for a moment. Lex quietly sipped his espresso and waited as if he knew Clark was sounding himself out. *If my father hadn't trained me to hide my powers,* would *I be out there lording it over all the ordinary people?* he asked himself.

"I don't think so," Clark answered finally. He locked eyes with Lex. "Have you ever kept sheep?"

Lex's right eyebrow quirked up.

Hah, Clark thought, *two can play this game of answering a question with a question.* "We did for a while — until they broke into the gardens and ate everything down to the ground. We had a border collie to help herd them.

"I remember when I was nine," Clark continued, "I used to watch the dog move the herd out into the pasture every morning. The sheep always tried to scatter, and he'd run in seven different directions at once and somehow keep them together and moving ahead. He was like a bolt of lightning in the field, and he never got tired. He stood guard over them all day, every day." Clark felt his cheeks go red, but he couldn't help it. The memory of that dog always brought a strange mix of emotions welling up, not the least of which was pride. "I thought he was so noble," he finished, "that I told my mother I wanted to be a sheepdog when I grew up."

Lex pursed his lips but made no comment on Clark's confession. Clark felt an irrational rush of gratitude that the twenty-one-year-old didn't make fun of a fifteen-year-old's fond memories of his childhood fantasy.

After a moment, Lex picked up his cup and saucer. Clark watched as he neatly set them back down in the center of the table. He picked up Clark's latte and placed it next to the espresso. Like a parlor magician, he smoothly exchanged their positions several times, round and round, back and forth. "Genetically, wolves and dogs are indistinguishable," he said as his hands moved. "They're both predators. In the wild, they both would eat whatever they could catch."

He stopped his game and lifted the latte. "Ultimately, a sheepdog is simply a wolf who chooses not to eat what it protects." He peered at Clark over the latte's rim. "So what is it that keeps it from turning on the flock?"

Now it was Clark's turn to ponder as he looked

from cup to cup. Finally, he said, "I don't know." He took his latte back and saluted Lex with it. "But . . . I'd still rather be a sheepdog than a wolf."

They sat and sipped their different coffees in thoughtful silence.

Chapter 4

The setting sun's orange rays made the Smallville Animal Shelter seem more like a furnace than a refuge of last resort. Heather was five minutes late for her volunteer job there, but still she sat on the park bench across the street. It was taking all her strength and concentration just to stay calm out there — and she knew she would have to be even stronger to go inside.

It's all those Kent people's fault, she thought, struggling to hold her anger and frustration at bay. *I go through enough pain working here, why do* they *have to remind me how much killing is going on around me all the time?*

She wasn't even in the building yet, but her skin already had that crawly feeling. *It's almost like my allergies are coming back,* she thought, resisting the urge to scratch. *But that* can't *be. They went away after I became a vegetarian.*

So she sat on her hands, fighting to hold her body still, trying like mad to ignore the waves of tingles that made her want to run a wire brush up and down her body, anything to make it stop. But she knew it would never stop. It would eventually get so bad she'd feel as if her bones were vibrating deep inside, and her head would feel as if it were filled with tiny bees, each with a tiny stinger aimed at a nerve. And they would start stinging and stinging and stinging and —

I can't deal with this! Not with the ghosts at the same time!

Moaning low, Heather snatched up her book bag and fumbled inside, feeling for the two objects that she always carried, the saviors of her sanity. There they were, the box of spinach-alfalfa tablets and the bottle of Green Heart juice blend.

Heather's life had changed the moment she'd discovered the Melville Farm's special selection of organic produce and juices. She couldn't imagine how she'd ever survived without them. A while back, when old man Melville's daughter Jodi had been hospitalized with a bizarre eating disorder, Heather had been terrified that her miracle cure would disappear. The Melville Farm had shut down and she'd lost all hope, especially when no one could tell her if it would ever go back into operation. Thank God it had reopened. Their special vegetarian products were back on the shelves and Heather felt saved.

She held her bottle of Green Heart juice up to the sunset, watching the liquid sparkle with its eerie inner light. *I can actually see it glowing with health. Why can't everyone?*

Quickly she swallowed several large gulps and wiped her mouth with the back of her hand. *"Ahhhh."* She followed the familiar warmth as it traveled down her esophagus and into her stomach, where it seemed to explode in a green flash that penetrated to the very cells of her skin.

The horrible itching, crawly sensation faded. *Too bad it can't make the ghostly moans of dead animals go away as well.*

Indulging in the sweet sensation of relief, Heather sat on the bench and gathered her wits. Then she hoisted her backpack and, squaring her shoulders, crossed the street and entered the animal shelter.

She survived the first two hours of her four-hour shift by grinding her teeth and concentrating on what the supervisor wanted her to do, one task after another — clean the cat cages, groom the worst of the inmates, wash down the dog runs, feed all the barking, howling, crying animals.

Now it was time for the veterinarian and the rest of the staff to go home, and everything was going to change. Now she was going to be the only one there. Heather was going to stay for two more hours before closing the place up for the night. And her two hours were going to be spent tending the injured animals in the hospital wing.

As always, it was a psychic wrench to enter that wing. The whimpers of the dachshund with the sprained back echoed hollowly in her mind, broken every few seconds by the groans of the mutt whose ribs had been kicked in by its drunken ex-owner. The collie with the burned throat never yelped out loud — only Heather could hear it crying, pleading in her head. At least the vet had medicated the German shepherd with the broken hip, whose moans of pain were nothing compared to the undercurrent of terror it sent out in waves, like a demented radio signal — with Heather a walking antenna.

Worse than any of these, though, were the cats, who refused to outwardly show the pain they suffered, but whose minds broadcast their agony and confusion with constant brilliant clarity.

It's all right, she thought at them, tears springing to her eyes. *I understand you, I really do. I can feel your pain. We're trying to make you better, can't you see that? Can't you understand that? I'm trying, I really am!*

But they didn't understand. Nobody did. That didn't stop Heather, though. No matter how much it hurt to work here, she *had* to continue. It was the only way to block out the *other* groans and moans of pain, those of the innocents who had died so long ago.

Why did you have to take me on all your hunting trips, Daddy? she wondered as she worked. "It's good for you, Heather" she remembered him saying. "Toughen you up for the real world." *But I was only twelve, Daddy! How could killing innocent animals make me, make* anybody, *strong?*

She'd always wanted to have a pet, ever since she could remember. Animals didn't judge. They didn't wish you were a boy instead of a girl. They didn't nag you if you were weak or yell at you when you made mistakes. They loved unconditionally and only wanted your love in return.

But Heather couldn't have pets. "They'll ruin the furniture!" her mother had said. "Pets are free-loaders!" her father had said. And the doctors? "Remember your allergies," they told her over and over. "It's not healthy."

Her parents just told her what a foolish little girl she was.

Then, after the green flashes of the meteor shower, things had changed, as they had for so many other people in Smallville.

Every night in her dreams, she could finally

touch animals, animals of any kind — cats, dogs, horses, birds, even wild animals. She dreamed of running her fingers through the tawny manes of huge lions, of being licked into frenzied laughter by a pack of gray wolves. Her skin still crawled when she touched them in dreams, but it was a good feeling this time, a feeling of connection, as if every nerve ending in her flesh rejoiced, and her skin wanted to burst open and let her spirit run free with the wild creatures.

And then, the most wonderful thing would happen — in her dreams — she would become an animal herself. She ran with the wolves. She flew with the eagles. She splashed in the sea with dolphins and whales. It was heaven! Until . . .

The dreams ended, Heather thought, trying to keep her hand steady as she placed a fresh bowl of water in the cage of a sick Burmese cat. *Why do all my dreams have to turn into one of Daddy's hunting trips?* She didn't want to think about it, but the dream images paraded through her mind and she couldn't stop them.

If she dreamed she was a bird, she'd suddenly

end up in the marsh where her father used to hunt ducks. If she dreamed of being a deer, she'd find herself in the woods around the Luthor hunting lodge. No matter where she ended up, she'd watch her father raise his rifle and take aim. There would be a *bang!* that echoed across the universe, and the animal would scream. Scream and die. And Heather would die with it, its screams echoing in her head.

I wake up in bed, sweating and clawing at my sheets, because the dead animal's screams are still in my head. Heather put a bowl of milk-soaked kibble in the cage with five quivering, mewling kittens, watching them tumble over each other in their eagerness to eat. *The screams never go away. They're still here, in my head.*

She'd tried everything to make them go away. She'd prayed every night, apologized to all her father's gruesome trophies in the conservatory — she'd even stopped eating meat and wearing leather. That had stopped the allergies, but it hadn't stopped the dreams or the ghost voices.

A loud thump at the back door made her jump.

A little puppy squealed, startled, as Heather quickly shut its cage and rushed out of the hospital wing.

The minute she reached the shelter's back door, she could feel it. Something was terribly wrong. A new whine of agony suddenly pierced her skull like a knife, and she gasped, knowing now what she would find outside.

Hand trembling, she yanked the door open.

In the eerie orange glare of the sodium-lamp security light lay a battered banana box. Crumpled within, not cushioned by a blanket or even newspapers, was a whippet. Heather was no veterinarian, but even she could see that the poor dog was horribly injured, probably from being hit by a car.

Heather couldn't look away from the awful sight. *Oh, God . . . oh, what do I do? The vet . . . I need the number for the emergency vet!*

Even as she thought this, she knew it was too late. She could hear the whippet groaning in her mind. It was dying. No vet could possibly arrive in time to save it.

"No!" she screamed. "Don't die! Please don't die!"

At the sound of her voice, the whippet struggled to turn its head toward Heather, locking its liquid gaze to her own. The movement caused the dog great pain — pain which Heather heard as a high-pitched keening that shattered every rational thought in her head.

Her hands acted of their own accord, reaching out for the dog. Gently but firmly she cupped the whippet's head, holding it still so that their eyes locked. She held its gaze, never blinking even as the spark of life in those soft brown orbs faded away.

In that instant, a flash of green energy tore through Heather's body, crackling along the surface of her skin with that all-too-familiar itching sensation. She howled in chorus with the whippet's death howl in her mind, feeling its connection to life break with a *snap!* that sent her own head whiplashing back.

This time the howl was her own.

Deep within, Heather felt her insides churning as if they suddenly wanted to be someplace else. The flesh on her arms literally rose in waves that raced up and down from shoulder to wrist and back again, while her fingers writhed like separate creatures all straining to break free. Her senses reeled, out of control, everything in her universe twisting and shrieking as she felt herself being thrown against some invisible barrier, thrown against it again and yet again — a barrier inside herself that stretched like a sheet of thin plastic each time she struck. Again she was thrown against the barrier, and then suddenly it finally tore open with a shower of green sparks.

Heather whined, crazy from the itching sensation that enveloped her body. She scratched wildly — and saw that her hands were no longer hands. Even as she watched, her palms shrank, thumbs receding, fingernails pushing out to become hard black claws. Her arms were sprouting coarse brown fur.

She screamed, only to find that her vocal chords refused to produce sound. She touched her face and felt her nose pushing out, farther and farther, becoming a long, pointed muzzle. Her ears tingled, and when she pawed at them they weren't human ears anymore. Her vision blurred, faded completely, and suddenly returned in monochrome. Before her lay a dazzling black-and-white world. Her nostrils flared, drawing in scents so complex, so exquisite, that she reeled, overwhelmed.

Hands and feet. She was on her hands and feet — no, her *paws* — while her back arched and swayed, finding new shape and structure, a new center of balance. With one final shudder she rid herself of the torn remains of restrictive human clothing.

What's happening to me? she thought, but the mind words sounded so far away, like a cry for help on a midnight breeze. *What are words, anyway? What are . . . whaahhhhrrr . . . ?*

"Grrrrrrr!"

Her voice, but not hers. A new voice, for a new body complete with new instincts and urges.

Heather's human consciousness fled to a tiny chamber in the back of the canine mind, where it huddled in terror, afraid to look out through canine eyes. The human girl mind hunkered down and gave the canine control.

It was there that two whippets shared the light outside the back door of the Smallville Animal Shelter. One lay dead in a discarded fruit box. The other stood shivering in the glaring orange light.

With a howl of pure terror, the live whippet ran off into the night.

Chapter 5

Clark was hanging with Chloe and Pete in the *Torch* office when Lana came storming in, steam practically jetting from her ears.

Chloe took one look at her and commented, "Whitney, right? I swear, the histrionics you dating types go through make me glad I'm an independent woman." She flicked a secret glance at Clark.

"No, it's not Whitney," sputtered Lana. "It's my Aunt Nell. Why can't she just let me run my own life?"

"Duh, because she's your parent — legally, anyway," said Pete. "They have a rep for doing stuff like that."

Chloe shot him a dirty look. It wouldn't stop him, of course. It never did.

Lana plowed on, ignoring Pete. "It was bad enough that she volunteered me and Whitney to emcee the speech contest." She caught herself, hedging her criticism of her aunt. "I mean, not bad, really, because it's a good way for kids to earn money." Her feelings kicked in again. "But she never even *asked* me if I wanted to do it. And now . . ." Tears of frustration welled up in her eyes.

Clark jumped up to put an arm around Lana, instinctively wanting to comfort her. Halfway through the move he bailed on it and decided to guide her to a chair instead. "Take a deep breath," he said. "What did she do that was so bad?"

Lana struggled to regain control. Normally, she maintained a cheery, almost stoic optimism about life — a direct result, perhaps, of the fact that her parents had been the first casualties of Smallville's famous meteor shower twelve years ago. The tragedy had shattered her life, turning the photo of her tear-streaked face, plastered on the cover of *Time* magazine, into a symbol of that remarkable day. That photo, which so eloquently captured the loss of one little girl, had inspired

Lana to spend her days in an effort to live life to its fullest, the way her mother and father no longer could.

Growing up in the next farmhouse from the Kents, only a mile away, made Clark her oldest friend. She had often told him many of the deep secrets of her heart. He was still, next to Whitney, her closest friend.

Thanks to Clark's association with the *Torch*, she had come to know Pete and Chloe. Pete was Clark's lifelong pal, and under that wisecracking surface, Lana knew there was a truly caring soul.

When she and Chloe had met, Lana had still been a cheerleader, part of the most elite and *in* crowd of Smallville High's girls. Chloe, being bookish and sharp tongued, had automatically assumed that Lana was a status-obsessed snob. But since Lana had quit the squad, the two girls had discovered that each was more than the other had assumed and slowly warmed their relationship.

Looking at their faces now, Lana realized that these three people were probably the only ones in Smallville to whom she could confess her true feelings. She took a deep breath and announced, "Nell entered me into the public speaking contest!"

"That's bad?" said Pete, honestly surprised. "I couldn't even start to list all the things I'd do if I had five thousand bucks."

Pete was sibling number six, the last kid in his family to get anything new. Most of his possessions, including his clothes, were hand-me-downs, some of them handed down more than once before finding their way to him. Even worse, his life was one big struggle to make his own mark on the world. In classes and in sports, he had to compete not only against his peers, but against the track records and accomplishments of older Rosses that many teachers still remembered fondly. To Pete, the idea of having anything brand-new, be it an object or a reputation, made him practically drool.

"I don't *want* to do it, Pete!" Lana exploded. "I have a ton of schoolwork to do. Since I have to emcee the thing, I still have to get an outfit to wear, not to mention getting a tux for Whitney! I don't have time to write and practice a speech before Saturday, even if I didn't hate the topic." Her beautiful face took on a bitter expression. "She *never* asks me what *I* want. It's *my* life, isn't it?" She turned her head away from them and stared out the window.

Chloe jumped into the silence. "Maybe I could ghostwrite you a speech," she offered.

"Only if Lana wants to be run out of town on a rail," said Pete.

Chloe clapped a hand on Pete's shoulder, digging her nails into his flesh. "Aren't you supposed to be on a sports field somewhere getting sweaty?" she said, a deadly sweetness in her voice.

Pete winced and squirmed out from under her grip. He got ready to smart-ass her back, then his eye fell on the clock. "Yipe! I *am* late for practice. Coach is gonna kill me!" He bolted from the room. "Later!" he shouted over his shoulder.

Lana continued to stare out the window. Clark looked helplessly at Chloe.

Chloe rolled her eyes and sighed dramatically. "Tell you what, Lana," she said. "I can't help you with your aunt, but I can go into town with you and help you shop for your dress and Whitney's tux."

Lana looked up in surprise, honestly touched by this. Then, doubt clouded her face. "But Whitney's at football practice . . . Anyway, he barely agreed to come for a fitting. I can't imagine him sitting still for shopping."

"Clark can stand in for Whitney," Chloe said, a wicked smirk on her face. "I'm sure if we beam cute-rays at him, he'd do the gentlemanly thing and volunteer to be our mannequin. *Won't he?"*

The girls made exaggerated pleading expressions at Clark with big Bambi eyes and much batting of eyelashes. Clark flushed to the roots of his hair and grinned stupidly. "You just want me for my body," he managed to say, hoping the words came out coherently.

"What else you got?" retorted Chloe. She and Lana grabbed his arms and hustled him out of the office.

ꕥ ꕥ ꕥ ꕥ

To Clark Kent, the next two hours at the Smallville Formal Shoppe were a blur of colors and fabrics, frills and giggles. The two girls paid absolutely no attention to his suggestions about formalwear — not surprising, since he didn't even own a suit, much less a tuxedo. He couldn't even name all the *parts* of a tux. No, he was nothing but a last-minute substitution.

That irony wasn't lost on him. Here he was, being fussed over by the girl he most wanted to be with, who was only thinking of the boy she most wanted to be with.

The worst moment came when the girls decided that his dark coloring was interfering with their color choices. Whitney was a blond, but Clark was "the dark, mysterious type." Chloe actually had the nerve to ask him to hold a photo of a sun-bleached surfer boy torn from a fashion magazine over his own face and think jock thoughts.

Clark drew the line at that. "No way — use your imagination," he said.

Chloe and Lana stuck their tongues out at him

in perfect unison, which made them all laugh. "Spoilsport," Chloe jeered, and the girls went back to discussing cummerbund colors.

Clark closed his eyes and let his attention wander. With his vision blocked, he noticed that his other senses ramped up to report on the unseen action. *Interesting,* he thought. *Even if you want to, you can't ignore the world around you.*

Not surprisingly, he found his ears identifying and tracking every moving object around him — the girls chattering with the sales clerk, the rustle of fabrics as shoppers flipped through the racks, the hum of the store's fluorescent lights overhead, the grumble of cars and the click-clacking of pedestrians' shoes through the open shop door. What really amazed him was that his nose was doing similar things on a completely separate channel.

The light scent of lilacs told him where Lana was in the shop, even when she went into the back room to inspect some special fabrics. Clark inhaled deeply, enjoying even this reminder of how, well, *delicious* Lana was to him.

For the first time, though, he noticed that

Chloe was wearing perfume, too — a rich vanilla-based scent. *Is that new, or has she always worn it?* Clark was embarrassed to realize that he didn't know. Maybe he should compliment her on it to show he'd noticed. *But if she's always worn it, I'd look pretty dumb for not noticing it before.* That was the trouble with girls, he decided. No matter what a guy did, he was in danger of messing up.

He was pondering how to get around this dilemma when a strong, musky scent suddenly announced its presence, wafting in from the street. The smell seemed familiar. Clark could have sworn he'd experienced it before. He opened his eyes.

Crossing Main Street just outside the shop, Heather Fox was heading for Mother Earth's Pantry, Smallville's only organic grocery. Clark knew Mother Earth's very well — the owners were major Kent customers, buying crates of chemical-free and pesticide-free produce every week. Just thinking about them made Clark recall the heady combination of earthy, wholesome smells that always filled their store.

Once he saw Heather, Clark recognized the

mystery smell as hers — after all, she'd practically jumped down his throat yesterday over Lionel Luthor's display. He knew that Heather never wore perfumes. She was too worried that they might have been tested on animals to determine whether or not they caused allergies. Heather had once shown Clark a book of horrifying photos depicting the rabbits most often used as test subjects. No, it was nothing stronger than pure glycerin soap for Heather Fox, and no cosmetics, either.

So what was that new undertone he was smelling? Whatever it was, it was making the hair on the back of his neck prickle. The very cells that made up his body were sending out a primal alarm, demanding adrenaline, gearing up and crying, *Danger! Danger!*

That was silly, of course. Heather might have the inborn power to irritate anybody within range, even the normally unflappable Lex Luthor, but what about her could possibly be *dangerous?* Clark watched as the girl disappeared into Mother Earth's Pantry, making the little bell above the door tinkle — a sound he heard clear as a . . . well, as a bell.

Clark closed his eyes again, thinking about Heather and how she'd gotten to Lex the Saturday before. Replaying the scene in his mind, he decided it wasn't surprising after all that Lex had gotten irritated with her. Lex made no bones about his tense relationship with his father. It was generally acknowledged that he was in Smallville as a form of exile as well as a test of his managerial skills. He also made no secret about his intention of proving his father wrong on this issue, in addition to many others. Father and son treated the tensions between them as a complex and challenging game, each move of their relationship expressed as a dare or a defiance instead of warmth and affection. It made Clark feel bad for Lex sometimes, but for Lex, it was just normal.

Clark thought of his relationship with his own parents. Martha Kent grounded herself with rock-solid practicality, but withheld not a drop of love or care from her husband or her son. And for all his strictness and avoidance of luxury and waste, Jonathan Kent knew that firmness always had to be tempered with sympathy and care. He'd never forgotten what it was like to be a young man stuck in a small farm town. If he put heavy restraints on Clark's use of his special powers, it was because he wanted Clark to realize that they came with heavy responsibilities.

I wonder what my life would have been like if somebody other than Jonathan and Martha Kent had found me? I could have wound up in an orphanage, with no one who cared enough to want me. It wasn't the first time Clark had speculated on his great good fortune, and like always, it made him shiver, just a little, to think of how lucky he was. Then again, exactly who *was* he? *Where did I come from, anyway? Who were my real parents? Did they have all the superhuman powers that I have? If they did, how did they use them?*

That thought brought him back to Lex's insistence that special advantages naturally led their user to lord it over those who didn't have them. *Is that really a rule of nature?* Clark wondered. *What* does *make a sheepdog guard a flock instead of attacking it?*

He suddenly registered Chloe's voice. She'd been talking to him for how long?

"Earth to Clark!" she said again, snapping her fingers in front of his face. "Yoo-hoo in there!"

"We're done, Clark," said Lana. "I've got to come back to take care of my own outfit later — I won't make you sit through that."

An image of Lana in the changing room flashed like summer lightning through Clark's mind. With quick embarrassment, he suppressed it.

"Let's go hit the Beanery so I can buy you a reward for your patience," Lana finished, unaware of why Clark's face had gone red.

"Yeah, maybe a little caffeine'll snap you out of your trance," Chloe added, poking him in the ribs. "Be honest, you weren't *that* bored."

Clark wisely chose not to answer that.

They went to the Beanery and, after settling in a booth, placed an order for the top ice cream confection, the Bucket Supreme. While they waited, Clark asked Lana the question that had been nagging him since she'd shown up at the *Torch* office that morning.

"Lana," he said hesitantly, "if you really don't

want to do this speech-contest gig, why are you spending so much time and energy on it?"

It was Lana's turn to hesitate before giving an answer. "I guess you could say that I owe it to Aunt Nell. She did step in to take care of me after my parents died."

Clark flinched at this. He still felt sort of responsible for the death of Lewis and Laura Lang — he'd always thought of it as *his* meteor shower, not just a random event.

"But what it really boils down to," Lana continued, "is that it's a job. A challenge, if you will. And I can't just *let* myself fail or even quit without giving it my best. It's not so much that I'm afraid of what Nell or anybody else would think of me, it's what *I'd* think of me."

And Clark, who felt exactly the same way about much of his own life, could only say, "*That* I understand completely."

Chapter 6

Heather left Mother Earth's Pantry without buying anything, without actually seeing anything, really. The whole world seemed unreal to her. She hardly knew what she was doing, where she was going, or why. She couldn't remember anything about the classes she'd sat through today at school.

It wasn't a dream, was it? she kept thinking to herself. *I really* did *become a dog last night.*

The evidence was undeniable. She'd come to her senses, naked and shivering, in her own backyard at two in the morning. With the doors of the house locked, she'd managed to crawl through an unlocked bathroom window and sneak to her bedroom for clothes before returning on her bicycle to the animal shelter.

There by the service door she'd found the tattered remains of the clothes she'd worn earlier — and the box containing the dead whippet. Sliding along the wall, desperate to avoid touching the box and its horrific contents, Heather had snatched up the rags and leaped into the shelter. She'd slammed the door, bolted it, and told herself over and over to forget she'd ever been out that door.

If anybody asks, I'll tell them the dog must have been left there after I went home, she'd thought. No one was scheduled to be at the shelter until seven the next morning anyway. All calls were automatically rotated to other vets for emergencies during night hours.

She'd blocked her mind of all thought after that, concentrating only on tidying and closing up the shelter, doing her best to leave no trace that anything out of the ordinary had happened during her shift.

The bike ride home and preparations for bed had been a mindless blur, as had school today. But now the enormity of what had happened was beginning to sink in. *I actually became a whippet.* Her body twitched a little as her muscles themselves remembered the change. *What kind of . . . of* freak *have I become?*

Mother Earth's Pantry was a mere six blocks from her Victorian-style home, and she walked to it in no time, her thoughts a jumble the whole way. As she approached the big, immaculately kept house, flashes of her dog-self's perception of the house from the night before flickered to life. To the Heather-whippet, this had been home because —

— it has my scent marking the territory. Sure, there are traces of other dogs on the picket fence, but none of them dared *trespass beyond it. Only a certain pushy tomcat attempted to do that — and* his *time will come the next time he shows up!*

Heather shook her head, clearing the foreign thoughts away, and realized she had to concentrate to even remember how to lift the latch on the gate. She entered the house and began trudging up the stairs to her room.

Then she stopped. Turned. Retraced her steps until she came to the one room in the house she'd always avoided. The room she had not entered since her father moved the family to Metropolis.

The room that had helped populate her nightmares for so many years.

She opened the sliding double doors to her father's trophy room. Taking a deep breath, she steeled herself and stepped into the stuffy, heavily curtained chamber. They were there, as she knew they would be, confronting her from all sides, studying her, judging her with their silent stares — dozens and dozens of stuffed wildlife.

Heather forced herself to face them. Bearskins and bison hides, complete with heads, carpeted the floor beneath her feet. The walls were crowded with mounted heads, hooves, and horns of just about every animal it was legal to hunt. One corner was reserved for the prizes her father had taken on a winter's trip to Australia in his youth — a kangaroo, some wallabies, a dingo, and even a Tasmanian devil. From the ceiling hung a preserved swordfish, souvenir of a deep-sea trip off the Bahamas.

Daddy meant to punish me by sending me from Metropolis to live back here with Gram. It doesn't do for a LuthorCorp vice president to have his embarrassment of an excitable daughter around when he entertains important people. No, send her back to live with an old lady who hardly ever leaves her room in the attic. Lock her up in a tomb filled with all those innocents he killed while he made her watch.

Heather approached the mounted deer head she'd always thought of as Bambi. It was so beautiful, with a sweet face that spoke of trees and dew and the solemn peace of the deep forest. For the first time in her life, she reached out to touch it, letting her hand skim lightly down its graceful neck, her fingertips whispering across what was once a sensitive nose. The green tingle from the previous night ran through her fingers as she stroked the stiff, smooth coat.

That's the same feeling as my allergy! she thought, suddenly making the connection. Now it seemed so obvious — she'd felt that green tingle all her life. It had always registered as a terrible itch, but now it felt different. Not painful anymore. More like an infusion of energy.

She pressed her hand more firmly against the deer's neck, and in her mind, Heather was pushed against that invisible barrier again. But this time the push was softer, more of a come-hither feeling than the frightening attack of the night before. Analyzing the sensation, she realized that the barrier was more like a door in her mind, a threshold she could cross voluntarily, if she really really wanted to.

She gave in to the feeling. Just a little, to experiment. She felt her body start to change immediately, watched as her fingers began to fuse together, hardening into a single mass.

A cloven hoof.

She gasped and snatched her hand away from the stuffed deer. Its glass eyes stared out over her head, oblivious to the miracle that suddenly stopped before it. Breaking contact with its hide had been enough to interrupt the transformation — Heather's hand was normal again.

Still, something was different, and Heather couldn't place what it was. She staggered back, her head spinning. Something had changed within her, but what? It took a moment to pinpoint it. When she did, Heather smiled.

The ghosts are gone. I don't hear them screaming anymore.

Relief flooded over her, but it didn't last long. One look at the beautiful deer and relief was overtaken by a tide of anger and resentment.

They're gone, but they haven't forgiven me. I still have to make up for what Daddy did. Heather swallowed back the lump in her throat. *But it's not enough to just try and teach people that they shouldn't hurt animals. People won't listen to reason. They have to be forced to change.*

I have to punish *them until they stop their cruelty.*

With new determination, Heather strode over to the stuffed razorback boar and placed both hands on it until she felt the green tingle, stronger than ever before. This time, she didn't try to stop the change.

CHAPTER 7

Clark walked down the front steps of Smallville High Wednesday afternoon to find Lex Luthor leaning on his silver Porsche Boxster, smiling at him.

"The way you keep showing up all over town, you'd think you never paid any attention to your business," said Clark by way of greeting.

Lex's smile broadened into a grin. "Clark, my man, when you get out into the real world, you'll learn that business isn't limited to specific times and places. Opportunities present themselves everywhere. You only have to recognize them and move when you see them."

Coming from anyone else, this might have been a casual comment. Clark knew Lex better than that. "Why do I get the feeling you have an ulterior motive for meeting me here?" he asked.

"Maybe because you sense an opportunity approaching," Lex replied.

Bingo! "Which is . . . ?"

Lex pulled a handkerchief from his pocket and pretended to wipe a smudge from the perfect finish of his Porsche. "It seems that a certain Smallville High jock has decided that emceeing a speech competition isn't in keeping with his manly self-image."

"Whitney's bailed on Lana?" Clark's jaw dropped. For Lana's sake, he always tried to curb his assumption that Whitney was shallow and self-centered. Now he felt truly surprised to learn that Whitney was actually acting that way.

"I believe his exact words to Nell Potter were, 'I've got better things to do than introduce wimps to a bunch of simps.'" Lex shook out his handkerchief and tucked it neatly back into his jacket pocket. He aimed a cynical look at Clark. "Poor guy doesn't realize that a course in public speaking would increase his chances of landing product endorsements after his athletic career fades."

For a moment, Clark imagined himself and Lana standing in front of an applauding crowd, as if they were being celebrated as Most Perfect Couple. Then he realized where Lex was heading. "Oh, no, Lex. I'm not going to —"

"Don't scorn an opportunity when it drops in your lap, Clark. You're the logical choice to be his replacement. Besides, the tux is on me." Like a stage magician, Lex produced a Smallville Formal Shoppe business card out of thin air. He held it out to Clark.

"Huh?"

Lex rolled his eyes. He spoke slowly, as if explaining something that should have been obvious. "I connected the Formal Shoppe with some designers I know so that they could supply all the gowns for the Fairest of the Fair beauty pageant. They owe me a few freebies." He walked around to the driver's side and pressed his security clicker. The locks of the Porsche clicked open. "Hop in," he commanded. "Your fitting is in fifteen minutes."

Reluctantly, Clark got in. As always, when he

sat on the slick, expensive leather seat, he felt like he was in danger of slipping right off as he buckled himself in. He kept silent as they pulled out into traffic, analyzing the "opportunity" Lex was offering him.

Where others preferred to take the easiest, least uncomfortable path through life, Lex went out of his way to find situations that challenged him. It was just like him to throw something into Clark's lap that would make him have to think hard about what he *really* believed.

What Clark really believed, at this exact moment anyway, was that his feelings for Lana were a constant, nagging temptation. Lex knew about that and was trying to help the two of them connect, that's all. Clark bit his lip, not sure why he should go along with it, except that it felt good to have a chance to help Lana out, like a knight helping a damsel in distress. What could be wrong with that?

Nothing, maybe, except that it made him feel a little uncomfortable, as if he were invading someone else's marked territory. "Were you serious when you said you believed that some people are born to be predators?" Clark asked, recalling his last conversation with Lex. "Don't you believe that choice has anything to do with it?"

Pulling out of a smooth left turn, Lex shot him a curiously amused glance. "You know, Clark, there are times when I envy your innocence."

That was nothing like what Clark had expected as an answer. "Excuse me?"

"You have two admirable people for parents. People who chose to have you as their son." Lex looked away, seemingly concentrating on traffic, leaving his words hanging in the air. Clark wondered what the point was. Although it wasn't a secret that he was Jonathan and Martha Kent's adopted son, the fact had long since faded from most of the town's memory.

Lex went on. "And despite your father's stubborn refusal to join the modern world, he does his best to make sure you're an ethical, morally grounded soul. If you turned out to be a threat to society, it would be because you chose it, not because he didn't raise you to be the best person you could be." Lex took advantage of a stoplight to lock eyes with Clark again. "So you see, choice does play a part."

Clark shook his head. "Sometimes I feel lucky to get a straight answer to a simple question out of you."

"Someday you'll realize that simple questions often have complex answers, and sometimes answers address questions you didn't know you asked." Lex said this as if he were talking to himself as much as to Clark.

They both fell into a thoughtful silence as they drove the next few blocks. Spotting a car pulling out of a parking space, Lex zipped the Porsche into it almost before the other car had completely pulled out.

"Here we are," he announced.

They walked into the Formal Shoppe. By now, everyone in Smallville knew the town's richest resident by sight. The saleswoman popped out from behind her counter like she was spring-loaded, ignoring several other shoppers who had been there before them. After conferring with

Lex for a moment, she ducked into the back room to retrieve the materials sample book and Clark's fitting info from the previous day.

The whole business made Clark twitchy. He hoped that the fitting would be over quickly so he could get back to the farm. Then he could think this problem through by doing chores, perhaps by chopping firewood with his bare hands — that always helped, for some weird reason.

Lex pulled out his Palm Pilot and began reviewing notes to pass the time. Clark leaned on the counter and, like yesterday, closed his eyes to block out distractions. As before, all it did was heighten his awareness of his other senses.

Someone in the store was sweating heavily. There was a sharp bite to the sweat, the kind Clark recognized from some of his classmates during pop quizzes or when someone was nervously lying to a teacher. *Fear sweat,* he thought.

He opened his eyes and quickly scanned the store. Two middle-aged men sat in chairs near the dressing rooms, pretending to flip through fashion magazines. *Just a couple of bored guys wait-*

ing for their S-Os to finish shopping, Clark deduced. *It's not them.*

A mother and daughter argued in whispers over in the juvenile section about the young girl's bare-midriff outfit. *Nothing suspicious there.*

A uniformed senior sat in a chair by the door, dozing in the afternoon sunlight. Obviously a retiree, he was one of dozens like him employed in Smallville as "security guards." *He's not awake enough to be sweating, much less be nervous,* Clark thought, mildly amused.

Over by the jewelry counters, a girl in Goth-wanna-be layers of black and ragged lace pursed her lips theatrically as she picked up, examined, and rejected costume jewelry from a tray. *I've seen her at school, haven't I? A soph, I think. But isn't she a little overdressed for this heat?*

It might have been a fashion statement, but the girl seemed to have taken the layered look to an extreme — and every layer had pockets. *That might account for the sweat. But what has she got to be afraid of?*

Then, as Clark watched, she picked up two

rings to examine, but only one went back into the tray. Her hands seemed empty. *Oh-ho! That was slick. No wonder she's all keyed up and afraid — she's shoplifting!*

The girl raked the store with kohl-smeared eyes. Clark flicked his own eyes away before she caught him looking. She stared hard at the door to the back room before turning her attention back to the tray. Her hands flashed, and more jewelry disappeared.

Clark focused his eyes to bring his X-ray vision into play. He had to concentrate to nail just the right intensity. Too little effort and all he would see would be inner layers of clothing — or an embarrassment of flesh. Too much effort and he'd only see things in the next building over. He was looking for the telltale signs of hidden metal.

Holy —! She must have half the shop in her pockets!

Her strategy in wearing layers was now obvious. With his X-ray vision, Clark could see that half a dozen of her pockets gleamed with rings, brooches, and —

How did she get that tiara *in there? The guard's not the only one who's asleep here.*

So he'd caught her in the act. The puzzle was — what to do about it?

I'm not a cop. I can't just walk up to her and make a citizen's arrest. Come to think of it, I'm not even sure what a citizen's arrest really is. But if I tell the saleswoman about it, she's going to want to know how *I know. Like I'm going to tell her, "Well, I saw her with my magic eyes."* I'm *liable to be the one they haul away.*

Maybe there was truth to the popular belief that people could feel when they were being stared at, because the thief abruptly turned away from the counter. She scanned the room again and, quickly again, Clark looked away. Then she headed for the door.

I can't just let her walk out with all that stuff. Think, Clark, think. You've got special powers — use them!

Whatever action he took, it would have to be something he could do immediately — and without attracting Lex's attention. Lex had a nose for secrets and Clark couldn't afford to feed his suspicions.

I've got to take my shot before she gets away. Wait . . . shot — that's it!

Acting as casually as he could, Clark reached for a couple of stray paperclips that lay on the counter. Palming them, he dropped his hand to his side and slipped the first clip between his thumb and forefinger. Trusting his aim and strength, he flipped the clip at the dozing guard's head.

The clip sped across the room faster than the — normal — eye could follow. Clark's eyes, though, watched it hit the security guard on the ear. The old man jerked awake and slapped at the stinging spot.

As the girl neared the guard, Clark flicked the second clip, this time as hard and as fast as he could. The clip hit the thief's outermost pocket and slashed through the gauzy material. With perfect timing, the cloth parted, and several bracelets clattered to the floor, practically at the guard's feet.

The man leaped up and blocked the door. "Hold on there, missy," he said sharply. "You got a receipt for those?"

Clark felt a flush of accomplishment and satisfaction. He had done the right thing and stopped a robbery, however petty.

I'd make a pretty good sheepdog, he thought proudly.

Lex had looked up at the guard's first movement. "So the old guy was on the ball after all," he commented idly. "I wondered if he was going to catch her."

Clark had to work hard to keep his surprise from showing. *Lex knew she was stealing . . . and didn't say anything?*

"Catch who?" Clark said aloud, not wanting to make an issue of it. "Did something happen?"

Lex looked sidelong at him. "You really need to learn to keep your eyes open, Clark."

CHAPTER 8

Heather walked through her father's trophy room, her hands idly stroking the stuffed and mounted animals as she passed. It had been a good, if tiring, evening so far. There was still one more trip to be made before she allowed herself to rest for the night. The question before her was which animal would be best for this last job.

As her fingertips ruffled fur and rasped on horns, brief flashes of each creature's energy flickered through her brain. Razorback, timber wolf, bobcat, mountain lion — each seemed to call out to her, inviting her to take on its particular shape and prowl the night.

Becoming a razorback boar had filled her with more power than she could have ever imagined.

She had been a small mountain of muscle, with wicked tusks and a fierce intelligence. But boars weren't built for traveling the long distances between downtown and the farms where her enemies lived.

Her experience as a timber wolf had been the most satisfying. She ran like the wind and struck terror into those cruel humans with their fiery branding irons. That same terror had provoked the strongest response, though. One of her victims had had a shotgun handy. Only a convenient bale of hay had kept her from getting a rump full of lead pellets as she'd fled the dairy farm. The sound of the gun had brought back echoes of her nightmares and had made her human mind run away inside her animal body. Only the wolf's instincts had gotten her out of there unharmed. No, a wolf was too recognizable by farmers with access to guns, and Heather never wanted to hear another gunshot again.

Her eyes fell on the stuffed dingo, mounted as if it were about to pounce on an unseen target. *Canis familiaris dingo.* Dingoes looked exactly like big dogs. In fact, dingoes were the ancestors of all six hundred breeds of dog. They had surrendered themselves to domestication earlier than wolves, but their association with man hadn't saved them. Dingoes survived in pure form only in Australia now. Even there, hunters and sheep ranchers were driving them nearly to extinction, calling them vermin.

Heather's hand cupped the canine's snarling muzzle. Dingoes mated for life. Somewhere, a litter of pups and their mother had waited in vain for this male's return.

You — and all the others — will be avenged.

No one would shoot at a big, friendly dog running through the night.

Heather gripped the animal's head with both hands and willed the transformation to begin.

An hour later, she turned off the main road onto Hickory Lane and loped toward the Kent farm.

It all started there, Heather thought, reveling in the sensation of her strong dingo body racing like the wind toward the unsuspecting farmhouse. *I owe it to those chickens to set them free.*

The thought of chickens distracted the dingo mind that shared her consciousness. That had been happening more and more often on this trip. Perhaps it just meant that she was getting tired. *After I free the chickens, I'll go home to rest.*

She had noticed that each animal she became had its own sort of ghost mind that thought along with hers. It was as if each creature's instincts survived in the cells of its skin and was awoken when she touched a pelt to transform herself.

To the dingo mind, the dark cornfields were filled with the most delicious distractions. Field mice, jackrabbits, and raccoons left scent trails across the pavement, and it took all of her human concentration to keep the dingo mind from leaving the road and pursuing every trail.

She came to the white-painted fence surrounding the Kent property. Looking at the house and barn through the dingo's eyes was like seeing them in a black-and-white photograph — canines didn't see color. They didn't need to. The world was filled with information supplied by other, sharper senses.

Heather hadn't seen the henhouse on her previous visit here and couldn't figure out where it was. The dingo mind had no problem locating it, however. To its expert nose, the henhouse was as obvious as a lighthouse would have been to Heather's eyes.

She trotted around behind the barn and stopped in front of the long, low, shedlike building. The door had a simple latch holding it closed. That might have been an obstacle to a wild animal, but not one with a human consciousness. She stood on her hind legs and flicked the latch with one paw. The door swung wide open.

Fly, be free! she thought at the chickens.

Nothing happened.

For a moment, Heather couldn't understand why the chickens didn't race out of their prison. She wasn't farm bred, so it took her a while to realize that the birds naturally spent the entire night sound asleep and weren't going to stir by themselves.

I can't wait for morning. They have to run away now! She thought a moment. *I'll have to* chase *them out,* she decided, and leaped into the henhouse.

With a predator in their midst, the chickens snapped awake and flew into a panic. Clucking and shrilling, they tore at each other in their haste to leap down from their roosts. Flapping wildly, they shoved and scrambled out the door, feathers fluttering like maddened snow.

All the excitement and bustle was too much for the dingo mind. Ancient instincts welled up in an irresistible tide, swamping the Heather mind. Her jaws snapped at flying feathers as her own awareness lost control and fell into an inner darkness.

When she came back to herself, Heather felt her jaws crunching on something. Her belly was full and her tongue thrilled to the taste of hot blood. With rising horror, she realized that she was eating one of the very chickens she had intended to save.

She tried to spit out the remains of her meal, but the dingo mind defied her. It took all her remaining mental strength to overpower her traitorous animal form and flee. Her last coherent thought as she reached the highway was:

Oh, God — what have I become?

ೞ ೞ ೞ ೞ

Clark clutched his pillow as he slept, oblivious to the holes his fingers were making in the pillowcase.

He was floating in space, high above a blue-green, cloud-shrouded globe — falling, falling. Only a thin shell protected him, first from the infinite cold, then from the rapidly rising heat. His view of the planet below dimmed, obscured by molecules of air that were being transformed into glowing plasma by the violent speed of his descent.

The planet below seemed to scream as he burned his way closer, piercing its protective atmosphere in a razor swipe, leaving black space behind and intruding into heavenly blue.

Farther he fell, a cosmic roar announcing his arrival, a boom like thunder announcing his landing. The shell that protected him burst open, and he squinted, naked and newborn, into the sunlight of an alien planet. Dimly he was aware of the trail of death and destruction he'd left behind. He had fled infinite death and destruction to come here, and it seemed only fitting the same should announce his emergence into this new world.

He felt himself grow taller and stronger as he walked to the nearest town. A smooth stonelike path lay before him, like a broad carpet of welcome. Large strange metal things on wheels sped toward him, blocking his path. He hit them with his fists. They crumpled at his touch, bleeding fluids and steam in their death throes. Their destruction gave him a sense of unexpected pleasure. It felt good to stretch his muscles. To test his strength, he lifted one of the metal things and threw it as far as he could. It shrank as it spun through the air, diminishing to a tiny speck before it disappeared over the horizon. He was strong, stronger than anything this world could pit against him.

This was good.

He entered a town and saw the beings who lived there. Most of them fled at the sight of him. Some simply froze where they were and trembled until he passed.

This too was good.

Delicious smells reached him, reminding him that he hadn't fed himself since his landing. He followed the aromas to a building where more beings sat eating cooked food. He approached the door, but the beings inside screamed, blocking the entrance with tables and chairs. Red rage grew within him. These creatures were trying to deny him what he desired!

He ripped the door from its hinges and threw it into the street behind him. Like a swimmer through a reedy pond, he waded through the obstacles the beings had piled between him and the food he craved. The food was laid out in metal pans set into a long table. He reached out with both hands to grab the food and cram it into his mouth. Juices ran down his chin and stained his hands and arms. It didn't matter — he was feeding, and that was very *good.*

A motion behind the table caught his attention. Something was also feeding there. Something as big and ferocious as himself. He growled a warning to his rival, but it didn't flee. Instead, it made roaring motions back at him, although it made no sounds. It was a creature out of a nightmare, with bulging muscles and a fearsome snarl on its greasy face. Food spilled from its open mouth as it chewed.

The thought of competition filled his veins with adrenaline. There was room here for only one to feed, to rule. He would prove to this rival that he *was the strongest and fiercest of the two of them. Without giving warning, he wrenched the table up and threw it at his enemy.*

When the table hit the restaurant's mirror, Clark —

— woke in a sweat. His pillows, the ones his mother had sewn herself and stuffed with feathers provided from the Kent farm henhouse, were in shreds. One of them had hit the far wall and burst into a cloud of fluttering white.

Chickens.

As the dream fright cleared, Clark heard the terrified cackling of chickens in the henhouse behind the barn. A quick glance at the clock told him that it was two-thirty in the morning. His father slept deeply, exhausted by a day filled with endless farm labor. He wouldn't have heard the noise.

Leaving a wake of swirling feathers as he ran out of his room at superspeed, Clark reached the henhouse in a single second. It took only two seconds to survey the area and find the bloody remains of one of their prize hens. Another five seconds — only because he had to be careful not to hurt the chickens — to gather up all the loose hens and return them to their roosts. Only after he had everything back in its place and had re-latched the door did he take time to think about what had happened here.

The raider had come around from the south side of the barn, through a muddy patch, leaving clear prints from that point on. The paw prints looked like those made by a dog. The prints led straight to the henhouse where a single clear print and a long smear crossing the latch told a strange story . . .

The raider had obviously stood up on its hind legs, one paw bracing its weight while the other *pushed up on the latch to open the henhouse door.*

Only after the chickens had fled their night-time roosts had the raider attacked and killed the unlucky hen. No dog, not even a wolf, would have attacked like that. They either would have tried to scratch the door open or attempted to dig under the wall. Besides, this was the middle of Kansas. Nothing the size of a wolf had ever been seen here, as far as Clark knew.

Clark realized that his nose was itching, as if it had information to add to the puzzle. He closed his eyes and let this secondary sense take over. Under the smells of churned mud and chicken panic was the scent of the raider — and something else, an oddly familiar deep, musky scent. With a shock, Clark recognized the second scent and where he'd last detected it — on Heather Fox, when she'd passed in front of the Formal Shoppe.

A blindingly fast speed-search of the entire Kent farm revealed no trace of Heather. The raider had apparently approached and left the farm along the main road, but unfortunately, despite how supersensitive his nose was at the moment, Clark still wasn't a bloodhound.

He stared long into the starry night, wondering what had really happened. When no answer came, he headed back to the house to wake his father.

CHAPTER 9

"*Y*ou're going to *what?*" Chloe spluttered.

"I'm going to co-emcee the public speaking competition at the fair," Clark repeated.

"With Lana," Chloe finished. It wasn't a question.

Pete clapped Clark on the shoulder. "Congratulations, my man," he crowed. "You're finally learning from me how to score with the chicks."

They were sitting together on a couch in the Beanery's lounge section, sipping coffee to stave off the dreaded three-o'clock slump. The hangout was bustling with the after-school crowd. Over by the coffee bar a small knot of noisy jocks in letter jackets was loudly predicting victory over Grandville in Friday night's football game.

"Actually, it was Lex's idea, not mine," elaborated Clark. "He was there when Whitney told Nell Potter that he was bailing."

Chloe had a strange, almost scornful look on her face for an instant. "Why is Mr. Lex Luthor looking for another do-gooder project in Smallville? He already has you."

"Be fair, Chloe. I couldn't just leave Lana in the lurch," Clark said plaintively. "I *had* to volunteer."

"How movielike," Chloe said archly. "Two people, side by side, bravely pushing on with jobs they say they really, really don't want to do."

"Come on, Chloe, don't be like that." Clark knew his attachment to Lana was an open secret, as was the impossibility of his ever being able to do anything about it. He didn't understand why Chloe got so touchy about it sometimes. To pacify her, he put his hands together in mock pleading. "Look, I need your help with something only you can provide."

"Oh?" She cocked a skeptical eyebrow. "I'm so glad I have *some* value to you."

"Oh, you do," said Clark, trying to sound earnest. "You're the town odd expert."

Chloe's bright expression immediately turned dark. Too late, Clark realized what he'd said — not so much what he'd said but how he'd said it. He stammered in an attempt to fix it too fast. "No, uh . . . I mean . . . okay, wait . . . I just wanted to ask, do you know anything about people who change into animals?"

The question penetrated Chloe's defenses, piquing that insatiable curiosity of hers. "You mean, like, werewolves?"

Clark nodded. He wasn't out of the woods yet, but at least she wasn't miffed anymore. "Sort of, I guess, but I was wondering — are there other animals people can change into?"

"Well . . ." Chloe's interest was fully engaged now. Her eyes narrowed as she sifted through her mental files, searching for data.

Clark's clumsy compliment about Chloe's expertise wasn't just flattery. No one in Smallville had a bigger collection of odd, unrelated facts in his or her head than Chloe Sullivan. No matter how obscure the topic, she was bound to know some tidbit about it — either that or she'd know where to find one.

Evidently her mental search was done. "Every culture has stories about skin changers of one kind or another," she reported.

"Skin changers?" The phrase conjured up an image in Clark's mind of flesh as a sort of reversible coat — human outside, furry inside.

"It's what mythology calls people who can transform into animals," explained Chloe. "Thanks to Hollywood, werewolves and vampires are well known, but there are lots of others. Most skin changers of legend were dependent on where they lived and what kinds of animals were nearby. For example, Celtic magicians who lived by seacoasts became seals. Russian warlocks turned into bears. The Norse believed in people who were really dragons in the spirit world. Locally, a lot of Native American legends talk about shamans becoming eagles, deer, or coyotes."

"Bet you really didn't want to know *this* much about it, did you, Clark?" Pete drawled lazily.

Clark ignored him. "How is it done?" he asked Chloe. "The skin changing, I mean."

"Usually it's an inborn talent," she replied. "That's just who they are. In other cases, it's a spiritual thing that a magic worker learns to do. They touch a totem like a tooth, claw, or pelt of the animal they want to become." Chloe looked full on at Clark. "Now it's your turn to answer. Why this sudden interest in mythology?"

"Because I think mythology may have become real last night and killed one of our chickens." Clark filled them in on the early morning's weird events at the farm.

Pete, ever practical, put on his big-doubt face. Chloe, on the other hand, took it seriously.

"You know, it's odd that you mention that," she said. "It hasn't had time to hit the papers yet, but my friends over at the *Ledger* e-mailed me about a sudden rash of reports just like yours in the last twenty-four hours." She ticked points off on her fingers. "Yesterday, Jack 'the Hog King' Kellner was driven into his own wallow by what he swears was a giant razorback. The wild boar went on to smash through several fences, scattering more than a hundred pigs. They're still rounding them up.

"Then a wolf was reported to have attacked the

Chavez brothers while they were branding cattle. Jaime Chavez has second-degree burns on thirty percent of his body after the wolf kicked branding irons and charcoal on him.

"And that's just the farm reports. In town last night, Helping Hands, the thrift store — you know, the one that had that vintage fur coat in its window — well, somebody, or something, crawled through a skylight and stole the fur. And the Hideaway leather crafts store was *skunked* so badly no one's gonna want to go near it for a week. Are you seeing a pattern here?"

"No, I'm not," objected Pete. "Look, break-ins are a dime a dozen in town — just check out the police log in the *Ledger.* And farmers around here are always complaining about something ruining them. It's what farmers do." He realized what he just said and quickly added, "No offense, Clark."

"You're missing a couple of important points, Pete," Chloe said earnestly. "Razorbacks live well east of these parts — and *wolves are extinct in Kansas.* The last one was sighted in 1905."

"Because people killed them off," snapped an angry voice behind them. "Just like they did the mountain lions and the bears. What's happening here is nothing those animal abusers don't deserve."

Clark, Pete, and Chloe turned around to see Heather Fox sitting in the Beanery's darkest corner, glaring daggers at them.

"Excuse me?" Chloe said. "You're saying all this is somehow *good?*"

Clark frowned. "Do you know something about this, Heather?"

She stared back at him defiantly. "I wish. Maybe the animals have finally had enough and they're striking back. If animals ever treated humans the way people treat them —" Heather's anger overcame her ability to speak. Her mouth closed tight, lips in a thin line as if words wanted to come out but just couldn't do it. Clark watched her cheeks flush bright red, like they had when she'd yelled at him in the school hallway for hanging posters. He'd never seen a temper quite like hers before. She was like a walking flame thrower just waiting to take aim.

Before Heather could manage the rest of her tirade, five jocks in red-and-yellow Crows football jerseys burst into the coffeehouse, elbowing each other and yukking it up. One of them hoisted a large, bulky object and yelled to the crowd, "Hey, everybody — check out Grandville's new Griffin!"

He held up a moth-eaten stuffed rabbit. Some wit had replaced its head with the stuffed head of an eagle and nailed the bird's wings into the rabbit's back.

"Dudes, you put the head on the wrong end!" somebody hooted.

Heather stood barely an inch taller than Chloe, but she threw herself at the hulking jocks. "You sick, twisted freaks!" she screamed, trying to wrench the bizarre hybrid from their hands. All she succeeded in doing was ripping one wing off before the jocks reacted.

Possibly they didn't mean to hurt her. Maybe it was just football reflexes in action. But one boy clipped the side of her head with an elbow check. Her lip split, spurting blood, and she fell, hit the floor, and tumbled behind the couch.

Pete threw himself against his angry teammates, trying to block any more violence. "Cool it, you jerks!" he roared.

Clark leaped over the back of the couch to help Heather. He was the only one in the Beanery who'd seen her eyes blaze green when she'd clutched the torn wing to her bruised face. Now as he knelt over her, he saw something he knew he'd never forget.

Heather lay curled on the floor, the torn eagle wing still pressed to her cheek — or rather, what used to be her cheek. Her face looked more like putty now, her features running like melted wax. Her hands shriveled up, shrinking back into her arms, while her arms flattened, growing wider and wider and sprouting feathers. Clark just knelt there, transfixed in horror, as her legs pulled up into her body until only two sticklike forms remained. Her torso twisted and shifted, a long sharp beak thrust through the flesh of her face, and in mere seconds, Heather Fox was gone, the only reminder that she had ever existed being a limp pile of clothes on the carpet.

In her place stood a magnificent eagle. It glared at Clark with fierce golden eyes.

"Heather?" Clark whispered, but before he got the word out, the eagle beat its powerful wings and lunged at him. Clark reflexively threw himself backward, and the eagle flew over him, heading up into the rafters of the Beanery. When Clark looked up, it was dive-bombing Pete and the jocks.

"Look out!" he yelled, but nobody heard. The Beanery erupted in screams and shouts as the eagle ripped at the jocks with its long claws and razor-sharp beak.

Clark spun wildly, trying to find something, some way to stop the rage-filled bird without exposing his secret powers. His eyes landed on a big, cheap rug of Elvis Presley — the "fat Elvis," of course — done in the style of a cheesy velvet painting. Under it was a banner that read, TELL EVERYONE YOU SAW ELVIS AT THE BEANERY! It was the favorite decoration in the place, but Clark ripped it down without a second thought and flung it across the room like a cloth Frisbee.

The rug landed over the cowering jocks, shielding them from the eagle. The bird shrieked its rage at being thwarted. Beating its huge wings, it headed back up to the rafters to find a new target.

Everyone else in the Beanery dived screaming for the floor, arms shielding heads. Chloe ducked under the coffee table only to find herself stuck there when everyone else hit the deck around the table, effectively trapping her without a decent view of what was happening.

All this confusion gave Clark enough cover to risk zipping across the room. On the wall behind the jukebox hung dozens of vinyl 45s. His fingers raked the wall, collecting a thick handful of the old plastic records. Dealing them out at superspeed, he flipped them one by one at the eagle like Frisbee artillery.

The bird shrieked its defiance even as it was forced to retreat from the bruising barrage of disks. With a flip and a dive, it swooped for the door and disappeared out into the autumn sky.

Clark wanted to rush out into the street to

track the bird's escape, but now that they were safe, people were scrambling up from the floor. In seconds he was surrounded by a crowd that thumped him on the back and practically deluged him with congratulations.

"Way to go, Kent!"

"Great shooting with the records!"

"Good thinkin', dude!"

Chloe crawled out from under the table. "Rescuing people is becoming your trademark, Clark," she said, surveying the damage with a frown Clark knew to be frustration — Chloe had missed seeing the fight, and she hated that. Clark couldn't help but be relieved.

Pete was the last to claw his way out from under the Elvis rug. He blinked in confusion at the chaos around him. "What the heck just happened?"

Clark had an answer, but he was sure it wasn't one that Pete would want to hear.

Chapter 10

In spite of clear weather all week, the air on Saturday morning hung thick and heavy, as if a thunderstorm hunkered just over the horizon. This did nothing to stop huge crowds from swarming to Swanderson Ranch to attend the opening day of the Lowell County Fair, however. Come rain or shine, the fair always drew a crowd.

"Half of Kansas must be here today," Chloe said, excited. "Wow, maybe we'll make the national news."

Clark seriously doubted that. He just nodded at Chloe, amused at the expression on her face. It was only a county fair, but she was gawking at everything, mentally recording every detail, and filing it away for future reference. Clark knew that Chloe was on reporter overdrive, already composing an article. He also knew that she'd be mortified to know that she looked like an excited kid.

Swanderson Ranch couldn't have contained the million-plus people Chloe estimated, but the sprawling complex, built primarily to host year-round livestock auctions, was certainly bulging with everyone from Smallville and most of the rest of the county. Hundreds of cars waited to enter the dirt parking lots, neatly filling spaces one by one as orange-suited teenagers earned pocket money as traffic directors. Dozens of temporary display buildings and countless food and craft booths had been erected around the only two permanent buildings on the property — Corn Hall and the infamous Meteor Museum.

Folks lined up at the balloon-decorated entrance gate to buy tickets. Clark and Chloe got in line, Clark waiting for the inevitable comment. And here it came: "Oh, God. Not that. Anything but that," Chloe moaned.

Clark didn't have to look to know what she

was groaning about. It had to be Colonel Korn and Katie Korn, the traditional fair mascots — in reality, two adults shameless enough to wear elaborate, foam-mold costumes that made them look like giant ears of corn. With feet.

Over his bright yellow bumpy body, Colonel Korn wore a cutaway coat and string tie. His huge foam face had round googly eyes and an absurdly stupid grin between a corn silk mustache and goatee. Whoever was inside had to peer out at the world through a small black mesh screen hidden in the colonel's open mouth.

Katie Korn, the colonel's bright yellow wife, wore a quaint '50s-style gingham dress, oven mitts — Clark couldn't hold back a snicker at that — and a pink-and-white checked apron, as well as a mountain of big hair.

Both ears of corn were handing out event schedules and special coupons as people passed through the gate.

After getting tickets, Chloe took a schedule from Katie Korn. "Love the 'do," she quipped to the person inside.

"Bite me," said a female voice from inside the costume.

"Shhh!" hissed the person inside the colonel's suit to Katie. "We're not supposed to talk!"

Chloe grinned innocently. "So tell me — how do you guys make baby corn?"

Clark snorted and pulled her through the gate. "You're in fine form today," he told her once they were on the main drag.

"I can't help it, Clark. This is just so . . . corny!" Only then did she realize what she'd said, and she burst into a fit of giggles.

Clark chuckled, trying not to feel too sorry for Colonel and Katie Korn. Truth was, he felt just as embarrassed as they probably did. Because the public speaking competition was one of the fair's first events, he was walking around in a dark blue tuxedo. "Have pity on the less fortunate," he muttered.

Chloe patted his arm, making sympathetic noises. "I'm sorry, Clark. I think you look dazzling. I bet Barbie will let you drive her around in her new Dream Car when Ken isn't looking."

Clark resisted the urge to deliver a friend-to-friend punch on the arm. With his superstrength, he was afraid he'd accidentally dislocate Chloe's shoulder. "Okay, okay, enough with the wise-cracks." *It'll be bad enough when I'm onstage in an hour, standing like this surrounded by a bunch of deer heads and elephant tusks. And Lana.* He gulped and pushed it out of his mind.

"So," Chloe said, "you've got an hour before the big event. What do we do?"

"Well, we could look for Heather," Clark said.

Chloe grew serious. "Has anyone seen her since Thursday?"

Clark didn't answer right away. During both of the previous nights he had made several super-speed searches of the town and outlying farms, looking for any trace of Heather. He hadn't found her. It was as if she'd flown away in her eagle form and vanished forever.

"No," he finally answered. "She wasn't at school yesterday, and her grandmother seems so spaced-out that she doesn't remember the last time she saw Heather."

"Look, I know I'm supposed to be the queen of weird," said Chloe, "but even I have a hard time believing that she turned into a bird."

"I saw it with my own eyes. And you saw the rips in that rug."

"Point, score, and match," Chloe conceded. "Still, to start on a rampage to punish 'animal abusers' and then just disappear — that's a job left unfinished. That doesn't sound like Heather."

Clark grimaced. "I know. And the longer she's missing, the more worried I get."

Adopting her usual flip attitude, Chloe chirped, "We'll deal with her when she shows up, then. In the meantime," she said and waved an arm at the fair, "what do we see first in this bucolic fiesta?"

Clark shrugged. "Whatever you want, I guess." He forgot that Chloe was new to the county fair. It was as familiar an event as Christmas or Halloween to him, but Chloe had only recently moved here from Metropolis. She'd spent most of her life in a city that was the ultimate symbol of sophistication and success compared to little hick Smallville. It disturbed him slightly to think of viewing his hometown from the other end of the telescope.

"What's in there?" Chloe pointed to a long, high tent on the south side of the main drag.

Clark hadn't taken a map of the fairgrounds from Colonel Korn. He didn't need one. The fair layout never changed. "The flower show's in there," he said. "It's kind of cool. Growers from all around set up exhibits. They get pretty elaborate, with whole minilandscapes with waterfall scenes and everything." He suddenly remembered. "Oh, scratch that."

Chloe cocked her head. "Why?"

"They hang water misters in there, to keep the air moist." He tugged the lapels of his tux. "All I need is to get covered with water spots."

Chloe shrugged. "Then what's in there?" She indicated another building.

"Home Ec exhibits."

"What, like, who bakes the best pie?"

"Yeah." When Chloe gave him an "I was making a joke" look, Clark said, "What?" feeling a little defensive.

"*Pie* judging? People actually judge *pies?*"

"Well, it's more than just pies. And it's not just girls. Guys enter things, too."

Chloe folded her arms, radiating doubt.

"I'm serious!" Clark said. "The art of making things at home is a craft to some, a serious business to others. Some people make whole suits of clothes, and there's a quilting display and table decorations and baked goods and —"

"Okay, I get the picture." Chloe thought a moment. "But Home Economics isn't my thing, y'know?"

"All right then, I have an idea. C'mon." Clark led her down the main drag.

"Where are we going?"

"You'll see."

Clark soaked up the happy familiarity of the fairground. Here was where the Orange Julius booth always stood. Over there Mr. Kay sold his homemade sausages, every year without fail, in his old-fashioned handmade cart. Larger stands selling hot dogs and aromatic Mexican food each had a shaded area next to it with plastic tables and chairs. By midday everyone would be circling those areas like vultures, desperate to grab a chair the minute a diner left. Sore feet often made for sore tempers.

All the booths, carts, and aisles alternated with the same surveyed precision Kansas farmers used in planting their cornfields. It all eventually led to the paradise at the far end of the grounds where kids gravitated like ball bearings drawn to a magnet: the midway carnival rides. From as far away as the main entrance gate you could see the giant Ferris wheel towering over everything, the calliope music from the merry-go-round, and the sound of joyful screams floating across the landscape like a siren song.

Clark wasn't heading there. At least, not yet. He led Chloe to a small booth. "One, please," he told the proprietor, and paid. "Here," he said, handing Chloe a giant stick of cotton candy.

She took it with a huge grin. "Do you want to know something odd?"

"I already do. You," he quipped.

"Ha ha. I've never eaten cotton candy before." Chloe studied it like a scientist studying a new bug. "Ever."

Clark grinned. "This I gotta watch." He laughed as she took a big bite of the spiderwebby stuff, getting wisps of pink stuck on her nose.

"Yum!" she finally said. "Kinda feels like I'm eating spun fiberglass, but it tastes good. Where to now?"

Clark looked around. The one place he wanted to avoid, the place he avoided every year like the plague, was the Meteor Museum's mineral show. He *couldn't* go in because, among the hundreds of gems and minerals, there was a large permanent display of meteor rocks.

Before the meteor crash, Smallville had proclaimed itself the Creamed Corn Capital of the World. Not the most exciting distinction, perhaps, but the town was proud of its farmers. Then came the autumn day that changed everything. People had died, property and crops had been destroyed, and lives had changed when rocks from outer space carved fiery lines through the sky before scattering uncountable fragments across the Smallville landscape.

Lana's parents had died that day. Nine-year-old Lex Luthor had lost his hair after being caught in a cornfield when a meteor had flattened everything within a quarter-mile radius. And Clark Kent had crashed to earth in a capsule from who-knew-where.

Some of the meteors that made the trip down with him contained strange green crystals. Chloe believed that all of the odd and inexplicable things that began happening in Smallville after that were caused by contamination by these mineralogical aliens. Clark agreed with her for the most part because he knew something that Chloe didn't — close-up exposure to those green rocks made him deathly ill. As a memorial to her parents, Lana sometimes wore a necklace containing a polished crystal from the meteor that had taken them from her. At those times, Clark's pain at being near her was emotional *and* physical.

He casually steered Chloe as far away from the Meteor Museum as he could, suggesting they go to the hobby show. "Pete's in there, isn't he? Let's see what he's up to."

Actually, Clark already knew. Pete had been in the stratosphere since the Crows' win over the

Griffins the night before. Right now he was over at the hobby show guarding the display of his precious baseball card collection and accepting congratulations from anyone who had seen the game. Clark would never dream of spoiling his best friend's glory by reminding him that, since Pete was third string, he'd spent the entire game riding the bench.

"Hobby show, huh?" Chloe said. "I was right the first time — this place is just plain corny."

Clark dodged and weaved through the crowd, taking Chloe's comment the way she'd intended it — not as an insult, but as a statement of surprise. She just didn't understand the locals yet as he did. Maybe by next year she'd understand what the fair really was — a joyous blowout for folks whose daily lives were often hard and narrow, and sometimes downright grim. A celebration of plain and practical people whom Clark was proud to call neighbors. *Just plain corny,* was it?

"Durn right it is," Clark drawled in his best corn-shucker accent.

Chloe looked at him wide-eyed, then dissolved

into another giggle fit. She grabbed him by the elbow. "Well then, c'mon, Li'l Abner. Let's find us our pal Pete an' git you to the fancy-talkin' show-down on time."

The path to the hobby show building took them close to the rodeo ring and its surrounding livestock show rings. "Now this section holds a lot of memories," he told Chloe. "I was in 4-H when I was a kid. Did you know that?"

"No, but I know it stands for head, heart, hands, and health. It's a youth club. Started in farm areas, designed to teach kids how to raise animals."

"I remember the year we had sheep," Clark said, "my dad let me choose a spring lamb and raise it for competition. I took care of that lamb every day, trained it and groomed it and even washed it with Woolite before the show."

"Woolite?" Chloe raised her eyebrows. "You're pulling my leg."

"Nope. Wool, Woolite. The lamb had to look its best in the ring. Anyway, I got a red ribbon and was so excited when the lamb got a good price at the auction. I completely forgot the fact that the people who bought it were going to eat it."

Chloe stopped dead in her tracks. "And you sold it anyway?"

Clark frowned.

"Oh. Sorry," Chloe said quickly. "Didn't mean to go all Heather on you. It's just that, I mean, how could you raise it like a pet and then . . . you know."

"My dad's a farmer, that's how. I mean, it wasn't easy, but learning stuff about life and death never is." Clark sighed. "I wish Heather could understand that."

Chloe spread her arms wide, trying to lighten the moment. "Let's find that corny hobby show building. Which way?"

"Past the cow barn." Clark grinned. "I bet you've never looked deep into a cow's eyes before."

Chloe folded her arms. "No, Clark, I can't say that I have."

Clark changed direction and headed for a long white building, beckoning her after him. "Let's walk through. You can't imagine how beautiful a cow's face is until you look at one up close. It'll only take a minute."

"Great," Chloe grumbled. "I get a personal viewing of the Venus de Moolo. Clark!" she called louder. "It stinks in there!"

He didn't stop.

"You'll get your tux dirty!" she tried again.

This time he paused. "I'll be careful. C'mon, city kid."

Chloe sighed. "If I step in something, you get to clean my shoes!"

CHAPTER 11

"Wish me luck, Clark," Lana whispered.

"Aren't you jumping the gun a little?" Clark whispered back. "There are still two speakers to go."

They sat on the Corn Hall stage to the right of the podium as the eighth contestant, Gloria Munroe, delivered her speech. She wore a long semiformal dress that seemed a little much for a speech, but Gloria had aspirations to be a businesswoman — "a female Lex Luthor." She wanted that prize money for college.

Lana had settled on a sort of junior power-suit look. The severe lines of her crisp slate-blue jacket and skirt were softened by a poofy lemon lace shirt. She kept tugging on the material that spilled from her sleeves and adjusting her necklace — a blue stone on a gold chain, Clark had noticed, relieved that she hadn't worn her usual green meteor-rock necklace. That would have been a disaster.

Lana looked tense and apprehensive, her eyes flicking to the judges' table where her Aunt Nell sat. Though not a judge herself, Nell had the perfect place to supervise the performance. "Trust me, Clark," said Lana, "I'm going to need all the luck I can get."

Her nervousness surprised Clark. She usually displayed such poise and confidence, even when she didn't feel it. As for his own nervousness, it had pretty much evaporated after the opening ceremonies.

Following a prepared script, he and Lana had begun by introducing Nell Potter as the event's organizer. Nell, in turn, had introduced her prominent guests, a county supervisor and Smallville's mayor. Each of them had spoken at length, praising everything — the fair, its organizers, the competitors, the sponsor, but mostly themselves, before turning the stage back to Clark and Lana.

Clark had let Lana do most of the talking as they formally announced the competition's theme and introduced the first speaker. Then it was just a matter of waiting five minutes — the required length of each speech — walking out onto the stage again, and introducing the next competitor. It no longer bothered him that he was wearing a blue "penguin suit" in front of hundreds of people. He just hoped nobody noticed the smudge on his sleeve from the cow that had licked him in the cow barn. He wouldn't soon forget Chloe's hysterical laughter over that.

The only negative thing about his job as stand-in emcee was the backdrop of stuffed and mounted animals. Clark had a lot of time to study it, and his opinion fell a little lower each time he took another glance.

Lionel Luthor's trophies were arranged in a custom display setting that had arrived from Metropolis by rail. Prefab sections were designed to fit together into what might have resembled a three-sided double-wide mobile home — if it hadn't been made of reinforced titanium steel. Luthor wanted no harm to come to his precious collection.

To that end, the display's front wall was actually a roll-up security door, also made of titanium steel. During setup, the tech crew that Luthor hired to assemble his portable museum had done a test run of the door's mechanism. In less than four seconds it had slammed down with a crash, sealing its treasures safely within. Clark recalled how the tech crew had spent so much time testing the door and adjusting the spotlights in the ceiling grid that they'd run late. The last man had barely scrambled down the ladder built into the display's back wall when Clark and Lana had stepped onstage.

Heather was right to be upset about this, Clark thought, still staring at the backdrop.

Every specimen was from a prized, rare, or endangered species. Exotic pelts covered the floor and walls like creepy carpeting and wallpaper. Herbivore skins from zebra, buffalo, and oryx lay side by side with predators like mountain lion and panther. Next to the patterned pelts of jaguar, ocelot, and leopard, a giant Indian tiger looked positively plain.

A magnificent male lion and a Siberian white tiger, both fully mounted, stood sentry at each end of the collection, while between them a snowy polar bear skin with the head still attached roared up from the floor.

Hanging from wall plaques, bison, grizzly, rhino, boar, and warthog heads snarled ferociously. Between them jutted a prickly forest of horns and antlers from elk, moose, ibex, deer, musk ox, bighorn sheep, and impala.

Centered on the back wall, the LuthorCorp logo hung framed by two giant elephant tusks. Below it stood that deceased animal's gigantic feet, preserved and mounted like four stumpy stools. Balanced on the elephant feet was an oversized replica of a five-thousand-dollar LuthorCorp check — the contest grand prize.

I guess a billion dollars can buy everything except good taste, Clark thought. He knew that didn't matter to Lionel Luthor. Lex had said as much the night before. They had been watching the Crows beat the Griffins when Clark had brought up the subject of the display again.

"You shouldn't let yourself get worked up about it," Lex had told him mildly. "It's not like my father is out to offend Smallville. It's a dramatic backdrop designed to be shipped anywhere. He uses it at speaking events where he wants to be especially intimidating."

"But why bring it here?" Clark had asked. "Transportation and setup must cost him ten times the amount he's donating for the prize —"

"Hundreds of times, actually," Lex had interrupted. "But Smallville will never forget who the sponsor was, will they?"

True enough, Clark thought, looking over at the judges' table. But while LuthorCorp might be represented by Lionel's ego onstage, his son was conspicuously absent. Nell had wanted Lex to be one of the judges, but Lex had declined. His seat at the table was filled by Chloe, who furiously typed notes on her ever-present laptop. She glanced up at Clark and gave him a quick thumbs-up.

Applause brought Clark back to the present. The podium was empty, which meant that it was time for him to introduce Lana as the final contestant.

They stood up together and walked to center stage.

Chapter 12

Heather skulked through the fairgrounds dressed in baggy jeans and a shirt, sunglasses, and her grandmother's wig. She didn't want anybody to recognize her, but she didn't dare take animal shape, not yet. Ever since her unexpected transformation at the Beanery, her willpower seemed thinner than tissue paper. It was all she could do to keep her mind focused on human thought and not the jumble of animal-sense memories that crowded her head.

One thought managed to rise above the clutter: *This is all Clark Kent's fault. All Clark Kent's fault. Clark Kent Clark Kent ClarkKentClarkKent* . . . The eagle Heather had become earlier didn't have her human awareness, but it had still known that Clark had somehow thwarted it, keeping it from turning its prey into screaming, torn flesh. Its fury had pushed the human Heather into a dark mental corner where she could only watch helplessly as the Beanery had been trashed. Then Smallville had slipped away far, far below as the eagle made its escape.

Hours, minutes, seconds — time meant nothing to the eagle, and this had further loosened Heather's mental grasp on anything familiar. Primal emotions had drowned rational thought as the eagle cut through the air. Seen through the bird's eyes, the atmosphere had become like an ocean, updrafts visible like currents, giving direction and support to climb ever higher into the freedom of endless sky.

From impossible heights, tiny creatures moving below had tantalized the eagle's interest. Small creatures on the ground, creatures to hunt and kill. Hunger rose from within and drove it to the woods. There were rabbits down in those bushes. Flesh. Blood. Food.

Realizing with horror what was about to happen, Heather-human had found the strength to claw her way back to the surface where the eagle's thoughts roamed. Still, she was too late to stop claws from extending as the eagle's dive dropped it like a hammer onto an unlucky rabbit. The rabbit's death scream had filled the air, sounding just like the scream of a terrified girl.

The shock had almost knocked loose Heather's hold on the here and now, but the kill also jarred the eagle mind long enough for Heather to snatch control of the body. However, instead of becoming human again, the eagle's grasp on rabbit fur triggered another transformation. Heather shrieked in frustration as her eagle body morphed into the shape of a rabbit.

Heather-rabbit had recoiled at the smells that immediately assaulted its sensitive nose. Sky hunter! Predator! And there on the ground, dead and bleeding, its victim, one of Heather-rabbit's own kind. The smell of eagle and the sight of death washed out all logical thought. Pure, overwhelming terror thrust Heather's consciousness back into its mental prison, and Heather-rabbit bolted from the grisly scene, zigzagging through the underbrush until it found a small opening between a juniper's roots. It squeezed through and huddled down in the safety of the dark burrow, deep underground where nothing could reach it. Finally, oblivion had overcome both the rabbit body and the human consciousness trapped within.

Now, hours later, Heather walked down the main drag of the county fairground, zigzagging much like a rabbit, desperately avoiding anyone's slightest touch.

She kept her head down as she walked briskly, heading for the livestock area, her destination the rodeo arena. Her dream had come true — the ghostly animal screams that had haunted her for so many years were gone. But now she had an acute awareness of all the living animals around her, and their needs and desires and frustrations pounded against her skull like fists.

With the experience of being a rabbit still fresh in her memory, she could feel the hundreds of rabbits hunkering in their cages in the Bunny Barn to her left, their simple thoughts concentrated on the unnerving lack of hiding places. The chickens clucking in the Poultry Barn filled her with a sudden craving for corn and fresh, juicy grubs. The goats and pigs in their show stalls radiated desire for their owners to feed and comfort them in these strange surroundings.

Heather's mind threatened to come unglued amidst the babble of tempting, confusing sensations. She stubbornly clung to one central thought: *Clark Kent. Rodeo. Clark Kent. Rodeo. Rodeo. ClarkKentClarkKentClark . . .*

Somehow, last night, Heather had forced her rabbit body to hop from the woods all the way back to her home downtown, in spite of the body's nearly irresistible instincts to flinch at every sound and flee from any unexpected motion. All she could tell about time was that it had been night, with dawn on its way. The rabbit body was exhausted by the time it squeezed through the fence pickets to her back lawn, so she let it crouch in the cool grass and feed before she pushed it the last few yards to the back porch.

That was when she had nearly fled in panic. Just as she'd reached her back porch, she smelled Clark Kent. One instant there had been a blur, then Clark was standing there on the sidewalk, squinting at her grandmother's house. What was *he* doing in her territory?

There could be only one answer. He was *hunting* her!

Then a blast of wind had bent back her fur, and just as suddenly as he had appeared, Clark had vanished. Sick with fright, Heather had let the rabbit's instincts take over to rush her toward the welcoming shelter of a broken basement window.

Only when she was safe among her father's old camping gear did Heather force herself to return to her human form. Naked, cold, and exhausted, she had crawled into a musty sleeping bag and drifted into a dreamless sleep.

She'd awakened later to discover that it was Saturday morning. She'd lost a day and a half! *And Clark Kent is still hunting me,* she'd thought. *Maybe the rest of the town, too. I struck back for the animals and now they want to punish me for it!*

This all started with Clark Kent. This is all his fault! Clark Kent, chicken murderer! He hung posters bragging about that wild-animal murderer, Lionel Luthor.

He's going to be at that abominable display today, probably laughing and joking about those murdered creatures behind him.

She had considered her arsenal upstairs, all those fangs and claws in her father's trophy room. There had to be something up there that would let her punish Clark Kent.

No, I can't use those, she'd decided. *Nobody will let a bear or a lion walk down Main Street. They'll take out the guns that everyone keeps hidden and shoot me. There has to be another way to get to the fair.*

The fair. They have animals at the fair. Big animals. Animals that everyone will be afraid of — even Clark Kent!

So here she was, at the rodeo, where there was a corral holding a Brahma bull just waiting to give her body a new form. The corral was tucked far away from the public areas of the fair. Rodeo bulls and broncos were far too dangerous to keep anywhere near the main drag. Only the most experienced hands were allowed here.

Heather watched the experts as they tended the animals. She had been forced to slink between shadows and hay bales to reach the Brahma's corral without being noticed. Oddly enough, reflexes from some of the animals she'd become in the last few days helped guide her maneuvers. She felt more graceful than ever before, and her stamina and agility had never been so good.

But even with those new advantages, she faced a daunting problem. The dirty white bull with its distinctive hump was standing at the center of its corral, far away from where she pressed against the railing. She couldn't possibly reach it in order to transform. At the moment she was hidden from view, but someone would surely spot her if she tried to climb the fence and go to the bull directly. Worse, if she tried that, the bull would probably just charge her. Heather loved animals, but getting trampled wasn't in her immediate plans.

Nooo! she thought frantically. *I can't have come this far just to fail at the last minute!*

A feeling suddenly rose in her brain, much like the strange green tingle that rose in her body when she touched an animal. It built up like an electrical charge until she felt as if her very thoughts were sparking with energy.

Help me, Heather pleaded, staring intently at the bull. *I need you!*

At first nothing happened. Then the massive head lifted from the hay it was munching. The Brahma stared at her. Slowly, ponderously, it began to move. It appeared confused at first, wandering from side to side, but it slowly progressed closer to where Heather stood. She remained still and waited until she could feel its hot, moist breath on her outstretched arms.

Its nose touched her hand, and the change began.

CHAPTER 13

Lana stepped up to the podium and stood for a moment in silence. She gathered herself, took a deep breath, and began.

"Ladies and gentlemen, distinguished guests," she said, gesturing at the display behind her, "*Man, Conqueror of the Wild.* What does that really mean?

"It presumes a separation between Man and Nature. Me versus It. Man versus Beast.

"Let's start with Man versus Nature. Since everything in the world is part of the powerful force of life we call Nature, Man cannot, by definition, be separate from it.

"Me versus It also misses the mark because everything in existence can be boiled down to this simplistic statement. Everyone and everything is a *me* which must look out at everyone and everything else.

"So this leaves us with Man versus Beast. Here, at last, is a statement with meaning. But is it the limited meaning attributed by our sponsor, or is there a greater meaning, one that we constantly have to review in order to define who we — Mankind — really are?

"I was told through a friend that it is Mr. Luthor's belief that life is an arena in which a man proves that he is the top predator. His actual quote was, 'the meanest SOB in the jungle, with the pelts to prove it.'

"Since Man is part of Nature, and one of Man's roles in Nature is as a killer, we can't dispute that point. In fact, much of our history is a record of how efficient a killer Man can be, whether his victims are other animals or other members of Mankind. Mr. Luthor is accurate on this point.

"But a question immediately arises: Is that *all* Man is — a killer, a thoughtless beast who slaughters anything weaker than himself simply because he can?

"Obviously, there is more to our species than that. We have the power of choice. We can choose to kill, or we can struggle against mere instinct and choose not to kill. We can even go beyond that and choose to protect and nurture.

"When I look at our county fair, of course I see people who raise animals to kill and eat. Everything kills and eats other living things to survive. But I see people who do more than that — people who care about leaving more behind in Nature than they take out of it. I don't have to tell you about all the good, positive things these people do. You only have to step outside this building to see it for yourselves.

"It is Mankind's gift and our responsibility to draw a line between surrendering to the blind impulses of instinct and overcoming them. Every single one of us has to do that every day. When we do it as a whole, we call it civilization. When we do it alone, we call it moral strength.

"Do we hit the person who says a hurtful thing to us? Do we run off the road the driver who thoughtlessly cuts us off? Do we destroy those who dare thwart our desires? Every day we are tempted, and every day we, hopefully, conquer those temptations.

"I was tempted when I was given the opportunity to compete for this prize. I thought, Wow — five thousand bucks! That could get me a great start at Metropolis University.

"But then I thought of what I would have to do to win that money. I would have to defend a topic I found I couldn't support." Once again, Lana gestured at the display behind her. "I would have to appear to endorse a display that I found deeply and personally offensive. And I would have to do all that, not because I believed in those things, but because I was offered a tempting opportunity.

"I also realized that if I gave in to temptation and competed in this speech contest, I would be hurting the chances of the other contestants — the ones who really want to win the prize and who don't have the opportunities that I do to find other ways of financing the future. After all, I'm still a freshman in high school. I have time to work and plan.

"And so, I decided that I would have to draw a line. I decided to resist the temptation to surrender to my base instincts and step firmly to the side of choice, no matter what it might cost me.

"Therefore, I respectfully ask the judges to withdraw my name for consideration in this competition. Thank you."

Lana heaved a great sigh of relief and stepped back from the podium, facing the stunned and silent audience. She glanced at Clark, whose mouth hung open in astonishment.

But before anyone could react, a Brahma bull burst through the Corn Hall's open doors and charged at the stage.

CHAPTER 14

To Clark's eyes the rampaging bull seemed to move in slow motion. He doubted that even he, armed with superhuman strength and speed, could stop a ton of fury-driven muscle bare-handed. Fortunately, the bull seemed to be steering clear of the audience.

Clark blinked. *It's coming right at* me!

Its smell hit his nose, and he realized something else with a start.

That's Heather!

Lana was cowering in fear between Clark and the bull, which was determinedly clambering up the stairs to the stage. *I've got to get Lana out of the way,* Clark thought. He would not allow her to get hurt, even if it meant exposing his powers to everyone in the hall. He leaped into action, his movements nothing but a blur.

The crowd was in full panic, people screaming and scrambling madly out of their chairs, shoving against each other in a frenzied attempt to figure out which way to run. The chaos and clatter distracted them enough that no one noticed Clark snatch up the polar bear skin and fling it around Lana faster than eyes could follow. Assured that she was sufficiently padded, he sped her out the door of Corn Hall, laid her on the ground, and zipped back inside to deal with the bull.

One glance at the stage told him that he would have to fight this battle alone. The LuthorCorp guards had been trained to deal with emergencies, but this was way beyond anything even Lionel Luthor could have expected. Shocked beyond the ability to move, they were just standing at their posts, gawking as the bull charged into the display area. They didn't even think to draw their guns, which suited Clark just fine — he didn't want Heather hurt.

He had little time to debate his next move. The

bull's invasion into the display space triggered the electronic alarm. With a *whoop-whoop-whoop* of its siren, the door came thundering down in its tracks.

Clark had less than a second to tuck and roll under it before it slammed shut. A dozen bolts shot home, locking the security door down — with him inside.

Him and the Heather-bull. It was like being locked in a cage with a force of nature. The bull's crazed eyes locked on Clark, and it lowered its head, snorting and pawing the stage. Clark had nowhere to go.

The bull lunged.

Clark tried to dodge, but the bull easily tracked him in the small space. The first graze of its horn on his arm sent an ugly wave of nausea through him. *Uh-oh — what if the meteor rocks did this to her? If she carries enough of that stuff in her blood, I could really get hurt here.*

The bull's right horn caught him just below the rib cage. The pain was intense. He glanced down, expecting to see the horn imbedded in his side, but only the tip pressed into him, hooking under his ribs. Despite the meteor rock effect, his invulnerable skin was still protecting him.

Taking advantage of its small hold, the bull jerked its head, yanking Clark up off his feet and throwing him straight into a wall. The metal bulged when he hit, and Clark fell heavily, crashing through the giant balsa wood LuthorCorp check and sending splinters everywhere.

Clark glared at the bull, forcing himself to remember that there was a human soul inside that bestial body, someone he had to subdue without harming or, heaven forbid, killing. Ignoring his bruised and aching gut, he grabbed the bull's head and wrenched, flipping the gigantic beast into the opposite wall.

The bull collided with the mounted lion first. The two creatures, one dead, one alive, smashed into the wall, sending a shudder through the entire display structure. Clark watched, holding his breath, as the bull scrambled back to its feet.

But it had touched the stuffed lion. Even as it stood, the Brahma changed shape, its flesh rippling. Horns and hooves disappeared, instantaneously replaced by a tawny hide, brown mane, and razor claws.

Clark had witnessed Heather change into an eagle at the Beanery, but that transformation had taken several seconds. The bull that fell now rose up as a lion, the shift having occurred in the blink of an eye. A huge paw slapped Clark to the floor, and the great mouth bit down on his head before he knew what was happening.

As with the bull's horn, Clark's invulnerable skin saved him from certain death. It was the lion who howled in pain as its fangs snapped in mid-bite. Clark ignored his own pain and pushed with all his strength, tumbling the lion backward. He leaped to his feet, preparing to face another charge.

How am I going to stop her? She has dozens of shapes to choose from in here. She can just keep coming at me until I'm forced to hurt her one way or another.

The lion had crashed into the display's far wall, knocking over the Siberian tiger and slamming face first into a leopard skin. As Clark watched in stunned amazement, stripes flashed up her paw that was touching the tiger while the rosette spots of the leopard appeared on her lion face. Heather's shape-shifting abilities were trying to accommodate all three animals.

She can't control it. She becomes anything she touches!

Heather's lion body recovered in seconds, but by the time she launched herself at the nearest elephant foot, Clark had a strategy planned. He gave her the time she needed to fully transform into a monstrous pachyderm before he acted.

As the elephant's shrill trumpeting shook the walls, Clark raced around the display room, grabbing as many trophies and skins as his arms could carry. Ignoring the lunging ivory tusks, he took up station in front of the elephant and waited.

The elephant loomed only a few feet away. It didn't have to move much to reach him. As it did, Clark kicked into superspeed and threw the trophies and pelts at different parts of its great gray body.

Let's see how you handle that!

As he'd hoped, each different part of the elephant's body tried to transform into the kind of animal that had touched it.

The elephant's trumpeting changed in pitch from fury to panic as its body melted into a patchwork of conflicting creatures. Its skin stretched and shrank, changing color and pattern over and over while fur shifted into feathers and horns and back again. Cloven hooves, talons, and paws erupted all over the body then disappeared again, while Heather's vocal chords bellowed and roared and bleated in terrified confusion. Clark stood transfixed at the gruesome spectacle of a body trying to tear itself apart in an attempt to be everything at once.

The strain proved too much for the poor human trapped inside. The tormented spirit surrendered, and moments later, a naked girl collapsed unconscious amid Lionel Luthor's ruined trophy collection.

Only after he was sure Heather was truly unconscious did Clark allow himself a moment to breathe. *Just two more details to attend to,* he thought.

He snatched up the mounted bison head and used it to smash a bull-size hole in the display's back wall. Then he scrambled up the lighting-access ladder and draped himself across the grid suspended from the ceiling.

CHAPTER 15

SMALLVILLE POPS CORN-COUNTRY TRADITION

A Smallville *Torch* Editorial

by Chloe Sullivan

Right up front I have a couple of confessions to make.

1. I fully expected the annual Lowell County Fair to be a celebration of all things corny and end with a contest that would determine which of our stalwart locals could bench-press a cow.
2. I was wrong.

You're reading it here, folks — I admit I was wrong about something. Treasure this moment, because it doesn't happen often.

The reason for my inaccurate prediction was that Smallville itself (a.k.a. America's Weirdest Town, a.k.a. Mutant Capital of the World) made its mark on the fair. Longtime *Torch* readers know what I mean.

Even before the fair opened, rumors were flying about Lionel Luthor's controversial display of macho ego — a collection of hunting trophies playing backdrop to a speech contest with the totally lame theme of "Man, Conqueror of the Wild."

Also before opening day, Smallville was plagued by an apparent animal uprising, in which local farmers and businesses were attacked by suddenly vengeful creatures. These included appearances by a gray wolf and a razorback boar — neither of which is native to Kansas or this century.

These seemingly unrelated facts came together on Saturday, when a Brahma bull mysteriously escaped from the rodeo and crashed the public speaking competition right after freshman Lana Lang's speech. The bull completely destroyed Luthor's in-your-face collection and nearly did the same to Lang and fellow freshman (and sometime *Torch* reporter) Clark Kent. Kent escaped injury by climbing up into the lighting rig until the bull tore its way out of the display and — surprise, surprise — disappeared.

The bull has yet to be found. Meanwhile, fair officials still insist that the only Brahma bull present at the fair never left the rodeo corrals. Totally weird, but oh-so-Smallville.

To top things off, freshman Heather Fox was found naked and unconscious amid Luthor's trophy pelts. Fox, whose animal rights agenda was no secret to anyone who knew her, is presumed by authorities to have been planning some sort of disruption of the speeches to protest Luthor's collection. A plausible explanation, maybe. But it doesn't address rumors of Fox's association with an animal assault (by an eagle, no less) on certain jocks at the Beanery last Thursday. And if she was just a simple protester, why was she bundled off, as so many of Smallville's stranger citizens have been, to an "unnamed facility" in Metropolis?

Two other unexpected items from this weekend:

Lana Lang, rumored to be a shoo-in for the LuthorCorp–sponsored speech prize, used her speech to withdraw from the contest. Her turnaround is rumored to have majorly ticked off a certain local power broker. The five-thousand-dollar prize went instead to senior Susan Gourley, who reportedly *can* bench-press a cow.

And in another animal-related story, local junior industrialist Lex Luthor added philanthropy to his résumé by announcing a major dollar grant to the Smallville Animal Shelter. The oh-so-modestly named Lex Luthor Humane Fund will triple the shelter's staffing and provide free 24-hour emergency care.

Rather than being a celebration of traditional Kansas corn, this year's county fair was a celebration of traditional Smallville weirdness.

Clark folded his copy of the *Torch* and looked out across his family's farm. Sniffing the air, he was glad to discover that his sense of smell now seemed no more sensitive than his other senses.

But even without using supersmell, he could tell there were chickens and cows to feed, crows to scare away from the corn, and hungry rabbits to be kept out of the vegetables by new fencing. Keeping a farm going took constant vigilance and hard work.

Beyond the farm were a town and a country he loved. He knew that dangers he couldn't even imagine could pop up at any time, threatening ordinary lives and dreams. And because he had special gifts — and, as his father constantly reminded him, the responsibilities that came with them — Clark Kent would do the extraordinary things it would take to protect everyone he could.

Being a sheepdog isn't such a bad gig after all, he thought, smiling. *There's more than enough to keep me busy for a lifetime.*

About the Authors

David Cody Weiss and Bobbi JG Weiss

Like strange visitors from another planet, David Cody Weiss and Bobbi JG Weiss fell into writing books, CD-ROM games, trading card sets, hundreds of comics, as well as advertising and commercial writing. David Cody Weiss was an editor for Disney Comics and a longtime letterer, working on many DC Comics titles, including some featuring the Man of Steel. Bobbi JG Weiss started out as a 4-Her, surviving many county fairs like the one in this book. She later earned an acting degree at UC Davis and now works as a writer.